not until you - special edition

corinne michaels

Editor:
Ashley Williams, AW Editing

Proofreading:
Michele Ficht & Janice Owen

Cover Design:
Sarah Hansen, Okay Creations

dedication

To Katie Miller & Mindi Adams—my clucking hens. This group of girls
represents us in so many ways. May we always have Friendsgiving and
enjoy irritating the farmers. I love you with all my heart.
Cluck. Cluck.
Cheap. Cheap.

one

. . .

Nicole

"DON'T you want to get married? Have kids?" my mother asks for the one hundred millionth time.

"Not exactly." I roll my eyes and tap my pen on the sketchpad in front of me.

"You infuriate me, Nicole!"

Well, right back at you, Mother.

You're not exactly a peach either.

Each time we discuss this, she says the same damn thing. It makes me wonder why she brings it up constantly.

I'm sure it's hard for her on some level. I am my parents' miracle child. After years of trying, failed pregnancies, and ten of Dad's mistresses, I finally came to life. She prayed for a beautiful little girl who would fulfill their lives, and then she got me.

The problem child.

It doesn't matter that I own the most successful interior design company in Tampa. She couldn't care less that I'm content, happy, and need for nothing. Nope. To her, I'm an unwed slut who is never going to give her grandchildren. A disappointing daughter with no hope.

"Mom," I say through gritted teeth into the receiver. "As much as I'd love to continue this conversation, which was long overdue, I really need to finish this proposal."

I have a huge pitch to a new client in two days, and I'm not even close to ready. Ever since I fired my other designer, I've lost a lot of business. It's been hell, but at least *my* clients stayed with me. Being worried about my business makes for a very cranky Nicole.

Thankfully, this isn't a completely cold meeting. I met the owner a few weeks ago at a conference, so we're kind of familiar, hopefully that'll help me win the bid.

"Just promise me you'll stop these ridiculous—whatever it is you do." She sighs, and her voice drops. "With multiple men. It's not normal. You need to settle down."

"Not on your life," I say to antagonize her. "Look, women don't need to get married anymore, Mother. Marriage is a business transaction, and I'm not for sale."

"You absolutely are not my child."

She only wishes. "Nope, I'm Dad's."

As soon as the words are out, I hate myself for saying them. She's been a great mother, a little overbearing and intrusive, but she loves me. My father is a hands-off man. I think it's been about six months since I called him. I make a mental note to do that. The fact is, I'm a little too much like him. I do what I want with whomever I want. He indulged a lot, and I followed in his footsteps. Life is about living, there's no reason I need to be tied down to someone who will only end up breaking my heart anyway.

"Well." She huffs. "That's not something to brag about, darling. If I were you, I'd rethink trying to be anything like that man."

She really does have every reason to hate him. He can't even spell the word fidelity, let alone practice it. After girlfriend number twelve, he decided it was time to trade up for a newer model. My new mommy is only six years older than I am and pumped full of silicone. Mom got half his fortune in the divorce, but it was never enough to put herself back together.

"I didn't mean that, Mom. I really have to go. Unless you want me to lose my company, be broke, and have to move back in with you? I mean, I'm sure you miss living with me."

She laughs. "Fine, fine, go work. I'm going to the club, I'd like it if you met me for dinner."

The clock reads two in the afternoon, and while I would rather cut my arm off than go to the club, I was a bit cruel to her and, as much as I like torturing her, I don't like hurting her. "How about I meet you at seven?"

I can almost hear the surprise through the phone. "Really? Are you sure?"

"If you'd rather—"

"No, no!" She cuts me off. "I'll see you then. Seven is great. You finish working, and I'll see you there."

"Only if you promise not to try to set me up with anyone!" I add for good measure.

"Anything you want. I'll see you soon."

She's a smart woman and disconnects the call before I can say anything else. The club is filled with members who come from old money and their single children. I can't count how many dinners have turned into me sitting with someone's son, who happened to be home from a business trip or who remembered me from when I was ten. The worst part is that most of the guys play along. They don't really want to know me or date me. They just want their own mothers' off their backs.

I've deduced that my reputation of being very . . . interesting in bed has followed me. However, the last thing I want is some stuffed shirt attempting his first taste of dirty talk. No thanks, I'll leave that to the men who are actually trained lambs. None of them are lions, but I'm damn sure the lioness.

I power through the next few hours, and before I know it, it's six and I'm going to be late for dinner. Today, was the day from hell. My new assistant called in sick, the patterns that I ordered for the new drapery in the offices I'm designing came in wrong, and I lost an account that I worked very hard to get. How was I to know her ex-boyfriend and I slept together and that was the reason he left her?

I hate days like this, but still, a promise is a promise.

Not wanting to piss off my mother, I decide to wear something that won't make her head explode like I did the last time. I grab the pencil skirt that goes to my knees, a red blouse, and pair it with the pearls she gave me for my sixteenth birthday. Seriously, who gives a girl pearls at sixteen? Not my father, that's who. He gave me a car.

Having divorced parents sucks, don't get me wrong, but I learned how to play them against each other very early.

As I get into the car, I start to wonder what it would've been like if they stayed together. I can't imagine either of them would still be living. Well, one would be living, they would just be in jail.

My phone rings and Kristin's name pops up on the Bluetooth.

"What's up, lover?" I answer with a smile.

Each day I thank the Lord that my three best friends still love me. Heather, Kristin, and Danielle are the best people in the world. People talk about only having one best friend, and I think it's such shit. I've known them since grade school, and through it all, we've remained close. Sometimes I'm closer to one than the others, but there's nothing we wouldn't do for each other. I'm not an easy person to handle, but they've somehow managed to see past my layers of bullshit and accept me for who I am.

"I'm just checking that you're still okay with watching Aubrey this weekend," she says as I hear Aubrey screaming in the back. "Hold on." She sighs. I know she's covering the phone, but I can still hear her threatening to burn stuffed animals in a fire pit or something. "Sorry, it's been a day."

"Noah isn't back from filming?" I ask.

"No, and the contractors are tearing up the kitchen, Aubrey is having a meltdown, Finn has locked himself in his room, and I need to meet with this possible writer."

And this is the best form of birth control I know. I love my friends and their kids, but I'm not in any hurry to have kids of my own. At this point, if I can hold off another few years, it won't be an option anyway.

"Do you want me to come over after dinner with my mother?" I say the last word as a curse. Sometimes I think that "mother" is the best curse word ever. *Mother fucker* and *son of a bitch* are both forms of mother, and both are almost as versatile as fuck—almost.

Kristin goes silent. She knows if I'm going to dinner it means that something happened or will happen. "Please tell me it's at her house," she finally says.

"Nope."

"Where is Esther making you go now?"

I groan. "The fucking club."

"Well, now you should definitely come over after." She giggles. "I can't wait to hear more."

I grip the steering wheel as I make my way onto the highway to hell. "I actually volunteered. She must've mind fucked me in some way."

"Probably," Kristin agrees. "She's always been good at that."

See? Even she knows my mother is a master in mental warfare. I'll agree to things and then have no idea why or when it happened. I've often wondered if maybe she hypnotized me at some point without my knowing so I would never outgrow her torture.

"Anyway, about Aubrey, why isn't she going with Asshole?" I ask.

Scott, Kristin's ex-husband, is now known as Asshole. There's no reason to call him by any other name. He is literally the biggest dickhead I know. Thankfully, she finally saw him for what he is . . . an asshole . . . and left.

I hate him.

I hate that he ever hurt Kristin because I sometimes think she believes marshmallows are unicorn poop. Her glass is always full, and he tried to kick the damn thing over.

Men like him deserve to be castrated. I'd be the first in line to volunteer to do it.

"Because he's busy, I don't know . . . you know how he is now that his slut is gone. Plus, anything to help Noah or me out, and forget it, he's got plans. Finn is going to his friend's house, so he's taken care of. I would normally just cancel, but I've already rescheduled on this girl twice. I *need* to hire another writer for the magazine. So, you'd *really* be helping me more than anything if you could watch Aub."

She doesn't need to say anything more. I love Aubrey. There is nothing I wouldn't do for that kid, she's my goddaughter, and I'm molding her into the little girl that will drive her mother to drink.

"I'm happy to watch her. It's been a while since I've had time to corrupt her," I tell her.

"Yeah, that's what I worry about. You did a bang-up job with Ava."

My other goddaughter, Ava, is Danielle's oldest daughter. I'm not sure what she was thinking when she picked me for that one. Honestly, I don't know what any of my friends were thinking when they made these decisions. They've known me since I was a teenager, watched me do things that make them wonder if I have any morals, and yet . . . they still let me near their children.

Ava is the best, though, she's fourteen and loves me. I let her do all the things her mother says she isn't allowed to do. She's a great kid. Straight A's, is on the competition dance squad, and still thinks boys are only good to reach things on the top shelf.

I was a little too timid with Ava.

I plan to rectify that with Aubrey.

I smile. "As you should worry."

A loud crash rumbles down the line a second before Kristin curses. "Damn it, I have to go. I love you."

"I love you too. Have fun."

"Yeah, loads," she says sarcastically and hangs up.

I don't know how she does it. The idea of kids is great, it really is, but any sense of self is lost. Your house becomes a sea of disarray with all their toys, you can't buy nice things because kids make messes, and they wreck your body. My body is a wonderland that I'd rather not have invaded—by a kid at least.

The drive to the club is short, and I almost wish I had more time to prepare myself for whatever idiot is going to show up at my mother's table. The valet takes the car, and I head inside and pray for a divine intervention.

I don't get one.

"Nicole, there you are," my mother says as I approach.

Deep breaths and don't be a smart-ass. Yeah right.

I smile, but more at the idea of *not* being a smart-ass than because I'm happy. "Hello, Mother, here I am in my glory—just for you."

She ignores my tone. "You're wearing the pearls I gave you."

I instinctually touch them. "I am."

I see the flash of joy in her eyes, and I'm glad I did it now. "Well, let's hope your attitude stays as beautiful as you are on the outside. Lord knows that mouth will start acting up sooner or later."

My attitude is never as beautiful as my exterior. She only wishes. "I missed you too, Mommy. If I'm a good girl, will you get me ice cream?"

"I should've given your father custody." She rolls her eyes and turns away.

I bite my tongue and head in to the dining area. Sometimes, it's too easy to drive her crazy.

The club is nothing short of beautiful. Everything is always in its perfect place. As an interior designer, I appreciate the fine details that were taken to make this place look upscale but still cozy. The colors are warm, the lighting is soft, and there are lots of crystals that send light beams all over, illuminating the space in a way that makes you want to look around.

"Nicole, is that you?" Mrs. Akins asks as if she can't believe her eyes.

"Mrs. Akins, you are just as pretty as I remember," I say sarcastically. She doesn't look good—she looks plastic. The amount of plastic surgery this woman has had is absolutely ridiculous, and I can't even imagine how much it cost her very rich husband. That's the thing about coming here, once you look past the furnishings, all you see is spit on a turd. "You look like you haven't aged at all."

She gives me a pouty-lip grin, and I stand there looking at her like she is crazy. Her lips don't even move, I'm not sure if she's taking a dump or trying to smile.

"Oh, Nicole. You're so sweet, I just love you."

"Aww." I give an actual smile. "You're not alone in that. Tell me, have you had any work done or are you using some miracle skin line?"

My mother senses that things are going to go downhill fast, so she decides to divert the attention and starts talking to her about her children. I stand here, as they chatter on and wishing I could be anywhere else.

I scan the room, looking for someone I know who can save me from the torment of listening to them, and then my eyes land on him. A man in a black suit with a crisp light blue shirt and a deep blue, that borders on navy, tie is at the bar, slowly bringing a glass to his lips. His shoulders are broad, his arms are thick, and there's a dusting of scruff along his jawline. Holy crap, that man is beautiful.

Like, I'd do him six ways till Sunday and twice on Monday.

I don't know how long I stand here looking at him, but my mother taps my arm, and I begrudgingly drag my eyes from the man.

"Did you hear what I said?" she asks.

"Sorry, I must've drifted off for a second. You mentioned kids, and I just zoned right out."

Mother gives me that nasty look that tells me, once again, I have disappointed her. One day, I'll do better, I'm sure. Or not.

"I said our table is ready."

"Lead the way," I tell her.

We sit, and I do my best to ignore the sexy man at the bar, but it's damn near impossible. Mother prattles on about various projects she's getting involved in, and I talk a little bit about the business. All the while tracking him as he moves around the room. Our dinner is overall uneventful and, honestly, very nice. She tells me a little more about the new wing they're putting on at the hospital when we're interrupted.

"Hello, ladies," a man I recognize says as he braces a hand on the back of my mother's chair.

"Hello, Ted." My mother's face lights up.

Ted? Do I know a Ted? I don't think so, but there's something familiar about him that I can't put my finger on. But I swear I know this man.

I stare at him, trying to place where we've met before. I rack my brain, but nothing comes up.

"I saw you here, Mrs. Dupree, and I wanted to say hello. Also, I couldn't believe it when I saw Nicole with you," he says with his eyes locked on mine. "Looking as beautiful as ever."

"Yes." My mother smiles at him and then me. "You remember my daughter, don't you? You two went out one time I believe."

He gives me this grin, and it hits me. Onion boy. I remember now.

"You guys had a great time if I remember." She continues as if I'm not seconds away from kicking her under the table. "I'm so glad you're here tonight so you can reconnect."

Ted's eyes meet mine. "I know I remember. Do you, Nicky?"

No one fucking calls me Nicky, certainly not a tool who actually tried to make me pay for not only my dinner but also his. "I don't."

"Oh, sure she does, Ted. She's just kidding. My Nicole has always had such a sense of humor."

I glare at the back of my mother's head, waiting for her to turn and look at me. She promised there wouldn't be any attempts to set me up tonight, but I should've known better. She can't help herself. After a few moments, she still hasn't turned, and I'm done playing nice. "Oh." I snort. "That's right." I smile warmly. "You were the guy who was cheap and whose breath smelled like onions."

That gets my mother's attention. Her eyes meet mine with the fire of hell burning in them. "Nicole." Her voice is full of anger.

"What?" I lean back, putting my napkin onto the table.

"It's okay, Mrs. Dupree," Ted says. "Nicole made me laugh quite a bit on our date."

If that's what he wants to call it, that works for me. Though, it wasn't a date nor was I being funny. I was being truthful.

I opened my mouth to say something, but the stranger I have been watching all night claps Ted's shoulder with a smile. "Ted and I should let you both get back to your dinner. We have a bit of business to attend to."

Holy fuck he has a British accent.

Take my panties now please.

He's even hotter up close. He's taller than Ted, but it isn't just his height that makes him imposing, it's everything about him. I have a much better view now, and I have to say that I'm loving how well he fills out his suit. I could tell from a distance that he was broad, but when he's standing before me, I can see I underestimated his size. I scan his body, down to his hand and find no ring.

Score.

"You can stay." I offer the sexy foreigner who I'd like to hang around a bit more. I've never found someone in this club so tempting.

The men who are good-looking are all idiots. Their mothers dictate their lives. Their fathers dictate their futures, and their future wives will be the accessories meant to make babies.

I'm not an accessory. I'm the entire ensemble.

He chuckles. "That would be delightful, but I'm afraid we would bore you with details of our business contract. I apologize."

"Shame." I give him my bedroom eyes. I'd like to do some business with him myself. "I'm sure I wouldn't bore you."

The sexy Brit smirks. "I'm sure you wouldn't."

"Excuse my daughter." Mother steps in. "I blame the wine she had."

Ted ignores the sexy stranger's pass on joining us and pulls out a chair. "Sit, Callum, one drink won't hurt us."

"Yes, Callum, please sit." I grin. Maybe dinner at the club won't be so bad after all.

two

. . .

Nicole

ONE DRINK TURNS INTO THREE, and Ted hasn't shut up once.

"Tell Nicole about your new job," my mother urges.

I fight off an audible groan. I wonder if eardrums can rupture from annoyance? If so, I'm on the brink of it.

The only thing keeping me from walking out that door is Callum. He's sitting beside me, not saying much, sipping his scotch with one cube of ice. But every now and then, his royal blue eyes meet mine, and I'm lost. I've never seen more hypnotic eyes before. His cologne lingers in the air around us, and I lean a little closer to him, wanting him to touch me.

"I'm managing overseas companies, helping them expand into the . . ." He keeps talking, but I zone out.

I try not to stare, I really do, but I can't help it. And then that voice. Not wanting to wait another minute listening to Onion Boy and his boring stories, I drop my hand to rest on Callum's and make my move.

"Tell me, Callum, what is it that you do?" I ask, stopping Ted's talking.

He gives an apologetic smile to Ted and then looks at me. "I own a real estate investment company. You?"

"Nicole is a designer," Ted answers for me.

"Thanks, Teddy boy," I say with acid in my tone. "But yes, I'm a designer. In fact, I own my design firm, so sometimes I get to . . . appreciate the finer details." I move my hand from his, letting my skin graze his a touch longer than socially acceptable. "And other times, I get to be in charge."

Ted clears his throat. "Don't let her fool you, Callum, Nicole is always in charge."

If I could stab him with a fork, I would, but then my mother would beat me for it.

"That must keep you quite busy then?" Callum asks.

"I make time for fun."

This man has sin, sex, and power exuding from him. I could drown in it and still want more.

"As we all should."

Yes, let's have fun, Callum. Lots of sweaty fun with some screaming thrown in for good measure.

"Tell me, are you in the States for long?"

He shakes his head. "Just another day or so. I'm here for . . . personal reasons, but I took a few meetings before I head back to London."

I run the tip of my finger along the rim of my wine glass. "What a shame, I would love to show you around."

Callum coughs and takes another sip. "I'm sure I'd rather enjoy that."

"Oh, I bet you would," I say before draining the remnants of my wine.

My mother clears her throat. "Oh, Nicole, they're playing music." They always do . . .

"Yes?"

"You and Ted should dance," she nudges.

If I didn't look horrendous in orange, I would kill her. First, she promised no setups at this stupid club. Now, I actually have a guy I'd like to know more about, and she's pushing me to Onion Boy? No.

Ted takes my lack of answer as a yes and gets to his feet.

Damn it.

"You know, I'd really love to," I say quickly as he walks around the table. "But I hurt my ankle today, and I don't think it would be a good idea."

He stops, and his smile falls. "Are you all right?"

"I'm fine, but it's best to stay off it, you understand?"

Ted nods. "Of course. Mrs. Dupree, would you like to dance?" he asks my mother.

"Oh, Ted," I clutch my chest in fake awe. "She would *love* to dance. She's been just dying for a dance partner. That is so kind of you to offer."

Now it's my turn for the glare. Turnabout is fair play and all.

Mother doesn't know how to be rude, so when Ted extends his hand, she graciously takes it. If I wasn't slightly afraid of her, I'd be rolling on the floor laughing. Serves her right, she can deal with his nasty breath in close quarters.

I sit here, in an odd predicament. I'm usually very blunt and have no problem coming on to a man. Sometimes, the hunter likes to be hunted, but sometimes, it's best to be the prey.

I guess my quandary really is whether I want to be prey because Callum is most definitely a dominant man.

He's the perfect guy for me, really. Doesn't live in the area, no expectations, and I would very much like to hear him talk dirty to me with that accent.

Callum leans back, and his arm drapes over my chair. "You could give him a little hope," he says with a chuckle.

I shift and run my tongue along my lips. "Why would I do a thing like that?"

"It's bloody painful to watch him try while you continue to smash his dreams."

"Then turn away," I suggest.

"But then I wouldn't be able to see you."

Well, how about that. "And that would be such a shame, wouldn't it?"

Callum's body turns, his deep blue eyes lock onto mine. "It damn well would."

We both stare at one another, and the air crackles around us. I can't remember the last time I felt like this—pulled to another. It's as if everything but Callum is gone, which is insane because I just met him. But there's something different about him, and his presence is larger than life. His lips turn up into a smirk as if he can read my thoughts, and I snap myself out of it.

I tuck my blonde hair behind my ear, fill my glass, and drain the wine.

Jesus Christ, when is the last time I felt flush over a man?

Not since . . . him.

Not since I was stupid and let my heart open to another only to end up crushed. I was a foolish girl who thought love could be enough. My world existed for only him, and when I learned the truth, I was broken beyond fixing.

"Where in London are you from?" I ask, wanting to get back onto safe ground.

His hand touches mine. "Piccadilly. Have you ever been?"

"Once right after college, but we didn't stay long. I remember loving it, though."

He nods. "I thought so." His smile is warm.

"Why is that?"

"Just a hunch." Callum finishes his drink and then spins the glass.

"A hunch, huh? That I would like London?"

Callum grins. "It's a place that a designer would love. If you love art, décor, and architecture, then England is a wonderful place. Also, you're beautiful."

I smile at the compliment tossed on at the end. "Am I?"

He nods. "Yes."

"Thank you."

"You're quite welcome. Tell me, are you planning to go home with Ted?"

I look up, meeting his gaze. "No."

He smiles slowly, and I fight back a shiver. I don't need to hear the words to know what he's saying.

I'll be going home with him if he has his way.

"Is there someone you'll be going home *to*?" Callum's deep voice warms me to my core.

My heart races as Callum watches me. Instead of saying a word, I shake my head. Everything inside me—my chest, my stomach, my muscles—tightens. When he looks at me, I can't breathe.

I need to say something. To figure out what this crazy attraction means or get it under control because this is so not me.

Before either of us can speak, a hand touches my shoulder. "Nicole?" my mother asks.

"Yes, hi." I turn to see her.

"I was talking to you." Her eyes move from Callum to me. "Did you not hear me?"

"Sorry." I shake my head, trying to erase the fog that surrounds me. "I was ... "

"Callum," Ted says with a bit of harshness, which I didn't know he had in him. I would be impressed if I didn't already think he was a total moron. "Would you help me with the drinks?"

"Of course," he replies back and winks at me. "Excuse us."

I watch them walk away, noting the distinct differences.

Callum carries himself with confidence, as if he owns the room, whereas Ted is just walking in his shadow. I've known many powerful men, slept with a few too, but there's something about him that I can't put my finger on.

Most of my friends would run from a man like him, but I'm not that way. I thrive on the power play. In both business and the bedroom. The thrill of the chase is what I long for. I once thought the picket-fences life was for me, but then I saw the devastation that happens when the reality of marriage sets in. My two best friends are divorced and the other one almost was, but they "worked it out" after a year of utter hell. What kind of life is that? Being with a man who treats you like shit, belittles you, and saddles you with kids so you feel trapped? No thanks. I'd rather be happy.

"Nicole, what exactly is your problem with Ted?" She just won't let it drop.

"You're kidding me, right?"

"No, I am not," she says with anger.

I'm not sure where she's confused. Ted is definitely not the kind of man I would ever be with.

"The fact that you think I would ever date a guy like that shows that you know nothing about me," I tell her with indignation.

"No, you'd much rather date a man like your father." My mother's eyes drift away as the sadness starts to overtake her.

"Of course, you would think that." She doesn't even know Callum, but she always assumes the worst of me. What she fails to understand is that I'm more like my father than any man I would ever date could ever be. My father would never be hurt by another human being. He's built walls around his heart, not allowing a single person entry. In both business and his personal life, no one has the power to hurt him.

"So you think Callum is like Dad? How? Why? Neither of us

even knows who he could be like because we just met him. But you thinking that I would date Ted leaves me wondering what you're smoking. I could never be happy with a man like him. Is that what you want for me, Mom? A marriage to a man like *him*?"

My mother shifts in her seat, trying not to appear as if she's shaken. "It's not like that, Nicole. All I want is for you to be happy, get married, have children, but you don't want any of that. I don't understand you."

And that is the heart of the problem. She doesn't care that I'm not the daughter she wants me to be. She doesn't see that who I am is exactly who I want to be.

I'm the girl that wants to live life to its absolute fullest.

I'm the girl who wants to be happy, no matter what that looks like.

I'm the girl who is seeking something but can't seem to find it.

I'm the girl who just wants to be loved.

I'm the girl who will never let anyone know that I'm a bit broken.

three

. . .

Callum

FUCK. She's absolutely breathtaking.

I didn't come to America wanting to find anyone. If I had my way, I would continue to just have my one-night stands and move on with life. Yet, here she is, making me wonder things I haven't wondered in a long time. I feel like a bloody fool for even thinking about Nicole like that. I'm here to bury my father, not sink my cock into an American girl. I need to keep my head straight, focus, and get the hell back home.

But all I've been able to think about since walking in the room is her.

I stand at the bar, trying not to look over her way, and fail miserably. What is it about this girl?

"So, do you think you will have the paperwork rectified tonight?" Ted asks.

Oh, the deal. I completely forgot about that. While I should have been focusing on making sure the deals with my father's—my company are secured, I've been making bedroom eyes with the blonde.

"I bloody well hope so." I laugh. "I assume the lawyers will get everything in order."

My eyes find her again, seeking her out without even realizing it. She reminds me of everything I lost once. Everything I hoped for with a woman.

I love a woman who isn't afraid to stand up for herself. Nicole definitely seems to be unafraid.

"Good." Ted slaps me on the back. "I'd much rather focus my attention on the girl I let get away."

He's an idiot. She wants nothing to do with him, and he can't seem to see that or, if he does, he doesn't want to believe it.

"Ah." I smile. "You fancy Nicole?"

"We have history," Ted explains. "It's just a matter of time until she comes around. She's sort of resistant, if you know what I mean?"

No, Ted, I do not know what you mean. She isn't resistant, she just doesn't like you.

However, it would be bad business etiquette for me to state that. So, I shrug.

It's been five years since I've looked at another woman in the way I look at Nicole. I don't know what it is, I can't explain it, but she calls to me. The way she tucks her hair behind her ear. The way she smiles when no one else is looking. The way her eyes follow me as I move around the room, and the way she tries to pretend she isn't watching.

I want her, and I know she wants me.

"That's interesting." I smile as I take a sip of my scotch. "I guess we weren't feeling the same vibes. American women must be different."

Ted watches me, smart enough to keep his mouth shut, but I see the hatred burning in his eyes.

That's right. You should hate me, because I'm going to get exactly what you want—her.

"Like I said, we have history."

One thing that Ted should know about me is that I always win when I find something worth fighting for.

The barman places the other drinks on the counter, and we make our way back to the table where Nicole and her mother are sitting. From across the room, our eyes meet, and we both watch each other as I approach. She doesn't have to say a word for me to see what's burning beneath her eyes—desire, passion, lust . . .

Ted brings the drink over to her mother first, which leaves me the opportunity to sit in the chair beside Nicole. As soon as I'm close enough, the air between us shifts, proving that my absence didn't lessen our attraction, instead, it brought it to a boil.

"I thought you got lost," Nicole says with a smirk.

I bring my arm around the back of her chair, and the tips of my fingers just graze her neck as I lean close. "I have a feeling I'd have found my way here eventually."

This game of cat and mouse is going to end very soon. She's about to find out that I don't like to toy with my food.

She shivers in her seat, and I'm thrown for a loop when Nicole drops her napkin, her eyes full of mischief as she bends to get it.

I feel her hand on my leg, causing my cock to harden as she moves up. "Sorry, dropped something," she explains to the table.

However, her hand continues to find its way higher. Fucking hell, this woman is forward. I feel her just brush against my cock, and I practically growl before gripping her wrist, stopping her from rubbing me off right here.

I run my finger down the back of her neck and whisper so no one else can hear. "Later, you'll pay for that."

She grins and raises her brows. "I'm counting on it."

four

. . .

Nicole

"WHAT THE HELL is wrong with me?" I ask myself in the mirror.

The entire dinner I've been playing this game, wanting the very thing he asked me, and instead of saying yes, I ran to the damn bathroom.

Going to Callum's place has been the damn end goal, but in my gut, I know this will not work out the way I hope.

I don't *do* more than one night. I do meaningless, emotionless sex with men who I will never think about again.

My heart races just at the thought of him. I hear his deep voice in my head. *"Come back to my room tonight, Nicole. I would very much like to fuck you into tomorrow."*

Ugh. That accent. It's impossible to resist. I know myself well enough to know that I feel more for this man before I've even kissed him than I've felt for any man I've ever slept with.

I've lost my fucking mind.

However, I don't freak out. That isn't my thing, and I need to just get a plan in place. Once I have that, I can walk away, chucking deuces into the air.

Step one, I need to get out of here.

I grab my clutch and peek out the door. Coast is clear.

Every part of me wants to march out there, face him, tell him that I'm no longer interested, but I'm not sure I won't end up fucking him in the backseat of his car. So, I'm going to pull a Heather—and disappear.

I move down the hall, toward the valet, but right as I'm ready to the turn the corner, Callum catches me.

"Shit," I curse under my breath and look for another option.

His eyes meet mine, and I know I'm screwed. I can either walk up to him, tell him I'm not going back to his room, and have him somehow convince me to do it anyway or I can do what any self-respecting woman would do and push through the doors to the kitchen.

Which is what I do.

Because I'm ridiculous.

"Miss," one of the wait staff calls.

"Ignore me." I smile as I keep moving.

"Miss, you can't be in here!"

I'm well aware of that.

I continue walking as if he hasn't spoken.

"Ma'am!" Another person calls out.

I'm now running through a kitchen to avoid a man. Someone needs to lock me up.

I smile and give a little wave as I keep heading toward the back. Kitchens always have some sort of exit, seems reasonable this one will.

"Miss." A waiter grips my arm. "You really can't be back here."

"I understand that—"I look at his name tag and try not to groan—"Ned, but you see, I really need to escape . . . my . . . mother, yes, my mother. She's driving me crazy, trying to send me home with this terrible man who smells like onions," I explain quickly. "I would really appreciate it if you just helped me out, I would forever be grateful."

I'm hoping he can sense the desperation in my plea.

He shakes his head, and I fear I'm going to lose this one. "Do you have a crazy mother?"

Ned nods.

"So you understand that if she has her way, I'll have no choice and . . . you know, I'm just trying to do what I can to avoid something I can't handle. I don't want to upset her because that comes with a lifetime of guilt."

Ned sighs and looks over my shoulder. "All right," he acquiesces. "I'll take you out the back exit."

Yes! Ned is great, Ted is a loser.

"I could kiss you, Ned."

He chuckles. "I don't think my wife would appreciate that."

"Well, she's a lucky lady."

We start to move through the expansive kitchen, Ned leading the way. The waitress carrying a tray of pastries eyes me.

Don't mind if I do.

I take one and pop it into my mouth, which earns me a glare. "That wasn't meant for you."

I shrug. "Sorry! I'm a stress eater," I mumble with my mouth full of the sweet pralines with candy coating.

God, that's good.

Ned's eyes are about to pop out of his head, I shrug, and we're on the move again.

We get to the back exit, and I breathe a sigh of relief. "Thank you," I say, touching his arm.

"Good luck."

The kitchen exit is on the back of the building, which is nowhere close to the valet. I clearly didn't think this through. I'm not sure how I'm going to get to the front, get in my car, and get away without anyone seeing me.

If my friends could see me now . . .

I step around the crap in the back, worried about my shoes and a little grossed out that the club my mother spends God only knows how much to be a member of has grounds like this. Of course, she'll never know because I'll be dead when she chokes me for this, but I'll be sure to tell someone before I die.

I pull out my phone and send a text to Kristin.

Me: If I die, know that the grounds behind the club are gross.

Kristin: Umm . . . why are you behind the club? I'm pretty sure Esther would never allow any kind of grounds exploration. More than that, you wouldn't either. What the hell is going on?

My mother is prim and proper. Everything in her life has order, except for me. I'm the wild card that keeps her young, at least, that's what I tell myself. My friends know that I may be nothing like her, but still, I don't do dirt or camping or any kind of climbing through shit.

This is a sad day that fear of feeling anything for a guy I don't know brought me to climbing over trash in my Manolo Blahnik red heels.

Me: Maybe I'll tell you when I get to your house. If I make it out of here alive.

Kristin: I can't wait for this one.

Yeah, I'm pretty sure this will be a story my friends torture me over for years to come.

I get to where the cars are, smooth my skirt, and try to fix my hair so I don't look like I just ran an obstacle course.

"Hey!" I call when I see the valet.

"Miss?" He looks around confused. "Are you lost?"

I sigh. "Listen, I need you to help me out. Here's the ticket for my car, would you be the wonderful valet I know you are, and get my keys for me?"

His eyes widen. "I could get fired for that."

"But I have my ticket, it's my car."

"Yes"—he looks up where the entrance is—"but club members aren't allowed back here, and you have to get your car from the desk."

Why does everyone here actually follow the rules? I'm just trying to get my stupid car and get out of here without having to face Callum. It shouldn't be this difficult to avoid a man who makes my loins ache.

I pinch the bridge of my nose and go with my best exit strategy. "Do you know Ted Edwards?" His lips form to a straight line, telling me he very much knows him. "See, he's waiting for me up there, and as you can see, I'm willing to go to any lengths possible to avoid him. Would you help out?"

He nods. "You can't tell anyone."

I smile, move closer, and touch his chest. "It'll be our little secret."

"I'm happy to see you lived," Kristin says as she opens the door.

"Bite me. Are you going to let me into your house?"

It's still weird for me to call it her house. This is the house that

Heather grew up in and lived in until she met her perfect man and moved to the rich area of town. To me, it'll always be Heather's house.

She steps aside, and I walk through the door to my second home.

I spent a lot of nights here as a kid. I had my first kiss in this backyard, learned to shave my legs in the upstairs bathroom, and found a warm place far away from the coldness my house emanated at the kitchen table.

"Well, well, well, look what the cat dragged in." Heather smiles, exiting the kitchen with a bottle of wine in her hand.

"Heather!" I squeal and rush toward her. "It's been too long, you bitch!"

She laughs, and I rock back and forth, holding her in my arms. "I missed you too, asshole."

"Why didn't you tell me?" I ask them both.

Kristin shrugs. "It's so much more fun this way."

"It wasn't for sure either, but Eli pretty much forced me out of the house after I kept complaining about how I missed my girls and hated his smelly boy friends."

I squeeze her again and fight back the tears threating to form. Today has been a little overwhelming for me. It's been years since I've thought about . . . him. Years that I've kept my heart locked up tight in the chains, refusing to let them even rattle. Then all it took was one look from Callum, and the chains could no longer hold anymore, and the links shattered.

"What's going on with you?" Kristin asks from across the room.

"Nothing," I fire back.

She raises her brow. "Really? Want to try that again without the bullshit?"

Damn stupid friends who know me too well.

"I would, but I have some guys waiting for me." I sit on the arm of the couch. "Can't stay long."

Heather and Kristin share a look, and then Heather nods.

Great. They're going to tag team me. Which normally, I'd be all for, but Kristin knows too much. She's the only one who has any idea about the things I've hidden for years. That gives her an edge.

"So, you have no good reason as to why you were behind the club?" Kris asks with a knowing look.

"I'd rather not talk about it," I deflect.

"Oh, honey." Heather touches my leg. "It's funny you think we're going to let this drop. Out with it."

I glare at them both, but they just smile in return. I often wonder why I talk to them still. They're nuts and intrusive and annoying and stupid friends who I love more than anything. Also, I'm pretty sure they feel the same about me.

"Yeah, let's hear it." Kristin crosses her arms over her chest.

Heather nods. "You know we'll end up calling Esther if you don't."

"Oh, that is a low blow."

They shrug. "And what will happen is that she will give us a much different version from the one you would give us." Kristin huffs.

"Which will lead us to need to further investigate," Heather tacks on.

"And then we'll be forced to come to our own conclusions after a lot of talking to people you probably don't want us to talk to."

Seriously? These two are no longer my friends. I'm going to find new ones who aren't overbearing assholes.

"Okay." Kristin grabs her phone. "You leave me no choice."

"Fine, I met a guy!" I yell and get to my feet. "I met a guy, and he scared the fuck out of me. I flirted with him all night and planned to fuck his brains out, but when the opportunity actually presented itself, I ran to the bathroom. I hid like a stupid girl, ran through the kitchen to the back exit, and then bribed the valet so I could avoid talking to him. Happy now?"

Both of them bust out laughing. They continue on for a while, giggling and having great fun at my ridiculousness. "Oh my god!" Kristin snorts. "You're as bad as we are!"

"Umm," I say with my hands on my hips as I look pointedly at Heather. "No, I'm not. I didn't scale a fence." My eyes cut to Kristin. "Or fall into a pool when I was shitfaced!"

Heather sits back, sipping her wine. "You might as well have, my friend."

I didn't sleep with Callum, I just got scared and . . . oh, fuck.

"Oh, for fuck's sake! I pulled a Heathergate!" I slump down. "I'm fucking ridiculous like you two!"

"A what?" Heather screeches.

I roll my eyes and then cover my face. "I wasn't scaling any gates, but I got scared and ran."

"Okay, but what the fuck is a Heathergate?"

"You know . . . a fuck and run. I think it's a great name. You screwed Eli and then climbed a gate. It makes total sense."

Heather gives me the finger, and then I cover my face again. I can't look at them . . . or myself.

Kristin laughs. "You know what this means?"

I slowly pull my arm down, meeting her eyes. "No?"

"You have a heart. You got scared. You're totally going to marry this guy."

She's lost her mind. "I am never getting married. Ever. I don't have a heart, it shriveled up years ago. And I don't get scared—especially of men. I like them so much that I often invite two of them."

I know they don't understand any of this, but it's who I am. I don't like strings or more than one-time things. However, I like being the center of attention. I like when two men are focused on my pleasure. When they go home and leave me sated and happy, I'm even happier.

"Yes, nothing like being the meat in a man-sandwich." Heather pours herself another glass of wine.

"Don't hate."

She grins. "I don't. I think you're crazy and hiding. So, what was it about this guy that made you run and climb over trash?"

It was everything.

The way he looked at me.

The way he stirred this deep feeling in the pit of my stomach.

The way he said my name.

The way I thought about something more than one night of unbelievable sex.

I believe that everyone makes mistakes, but when you purposely follow the same track that led you down a bad road, that's insanity. I'm not insane.

"It wasn't just him, it was Esther too."

Kristin studies me, and I know she isn't buying it. Heather was always the more gullible one. "I almost believed you," she challenges. "But you don't back away from Esther. You don't run, and you sure as hell don't ruin thousand-dollar shoes over her. Try again."

I look down at my pretty shoes, touching them and telling them I'm sorry. My friends may make fun of me or not always understand me, but they love me. I've never doubted that. There are just some things I can't tell them, and this is one.

Instead of lying, I give Kristin a small shake of my head, knowing she'll understand.

Her eyes tell me she received my message and turns back to Heather. "It's clear she's not going to tell us." She purses her lips.

"Tell me more about this Heathergate situation. It's been a while since we laughed over your crazy antics regarding Eli."

When Kristin looks back at me, I mouth, *Thank you*, and she winks.

I may have gotten off the hook tonight, but there's no way this is going to be the last of this conversation.

five

...

Nicole

"KIM," I call to my assistant. "Can you make sure we're ready for the Dovetail Enterprises in the conference room?"

The meeting is in an hour, and I'm not even close to prepared. All Martin told me was that he has a large budget and wants the designs for his new luxury apartments to be impressive.

I explained when we had drinks that I can do impressive, now I have to deliver.

The issue is that I've gotten half information and a possible floor plan. It's really hard to make a design when you have no clue if the kitchen island is ten feet or four. Regardless, I'm a goddamn professional, and I'll do the best to show I can think on my feet.

At least, that's the lie I'm feeding myself.

Kim walks in, sniffling because I told her I didn't care if she was sick or half dead, she was coming to work today. "I don't know if we're ready."

I sigh and walk over to her, place my hands on her shoulders, and speak softly. "I know you're not feeling well, but this? This is game day. Do you know what winners do on game day?"

Her eyes close a little, but then she pushes them back open. "Win?"

"That's right. Are we winners?"

"I guess."

"No." I sigh. "We are. We're winners, and we need to get our asses in gear, okay?"

"Nicole, I'm dying."

She sure looks like it. "You're not," I assure her. "You look like you're ready to tackle the . . . umm . . . something."

Kim glares at me and then sneezes. "I'm ready to tackle a nap."

"Well, I promise I'll redesign your apartment if you can at least give me another thirty minutes of work." Bribery isn't my go-to, but I'm desperate.

Two nights ago set me back. I had planned to work for a bit when I got home from dinner, but that didn't happen. Instead, I drew photos of a chiseled jaw, light brown hair, and blue eyes. Each contour of his face was perfect. Each line was etched into my memory. And then I had to get myself off with my trusty bullet.

Work was not happening.

Ten minutes later, Kim returns, closing the door behind her with panic on her face.

"What's wrong?"

"He's early," she says.

"What?"

"He's here!"

I look at my clock and start to panic. "Shit. I'm not ready! We're not even close to ready." I start to gather papers into some sort of order. "He's not early, he's like a half day early."

I had hours still. Damn it.

Kim heads over and starts to assemble a folder. "I'll do the presentation documents. Can you stall him?"

"I can try."

"Oh, Nic, he's hot too."

I roll my eyes. "He's like a hundred! He's not hot."

"Well, he's ridiculously hot for being a hundred."

Jesus.

"This is irrelevant, and you have issues." I huff as I grab one of the designs that was sitting on the floor. I may have to go with this one, and I hate it.

God, why do people show up this early? Now I look like an asshole, and I'll probably lose the damn project.

I have one chance to show Martin Dovetail that I can do this. I will not fuck it up. I can't.

"What else do you need?" Kim asks.

"Grab those and go put him in the conference room. Tell them I'm on a call with another appointment," I instruct.

"I'll try to stall as much as I can."

"Good, get me at least ten minutes. Go!" I order her out the door.

This economy is scary as hell for real estate, and for designers, it's even worse. Some months, we're so slammed we can't keep up, and then others, I'm twiddling my thumbs. It's truly feast or famine, but I'm praying this one lands us a series of jobs.

Dovetail is new to Tampa, but they've been in Florida the last few years. From what I can tell, they're a Georgia based company and have been branching out into other markets. I met with Martin a few months ago, but then I hadn't heard anything, so I figured he'd forgotten about me. Two weeks ago, I got a call that he would be in town and wanted a meeting.

I was faxed over the details of what he was looking for in a bid on and almost died. This would be everything for my company.

I grab the rest of the papers and pray that what I have will be impressive enough for a second meeting.

Kim comes back in, helps a little, and grabs my arm as we walk out. "Listen, you're going to do great. Even on your worst day, you're better than any other designer. Call me when you're done. If I don't answer, it's because I've died from this head cold. Go be bad ass, and seriously, prepare yourself for a really hot guy."

I groan. "Kim, shut up. He's not hot the guy is freaking old!"

"Whatever you say. I got twenty bucks that says you're dropping your panties before the end of the meeting."

Not only am I slightly disturbed that she thinks the old guy is hot, but she knows this is my one rule in this business. I don't sleep with clients. Ever. I did it once, and it was a freaking disaster after. I ended up walking off the job and away from money I definitely needed at the time.

"Okay, do I have anything in my teeth?" I ask as I show her my grill.

"Nope. Perk your breasts."

I give the girls a little fluff, shake my hair back, square my shoulders and saunter out of the room.

In my mind, I go over the designs, pitches, options for changes, and wish I had called one of my typical hookups so I could've worked off some of this nervous energy, but no, I couldn't bring myself to do it.

Because I'm an idiot and having some sort of mid-life crisis.

I push open the conference room door with a smile that dies as soon as my eyes find the man sitting in the chair. "Mr . . . Callum?"

He stands with a wide grin and his hand extended. "Hello, Ms. Dupree. It's nice to see you again."

"Right, but . . ." I'm so confused. I met Martin. I had dinner with the man, and he didn't have a sexy British accent, big, strong shoulders, or a body like a god. He was small, irritating, but loaded, and was going to give me two plus years' worth of work. "Is someone else coming? I mean, you're not . . . I'm supposed to be meeting . . ."

"Martin Dovetail? No. I'm not him. I'm his bastard son who now owns this company."

"I don't understand."

Callum brushes his hair back and then takes a seat. "Martin Dovetail died. Now you have to impress me if you want the job."

And the floor drops out from under me.

I'm so fucked—and not in the good way.

six

...

Callum

ALL I CAN THINK IS: *Thanks, Father*. Over and over in my mind. This is the only nice thing the bastard ever did for me. It didn't click the other day when I heard her name. Honestly, I'd just spent three hours listening to employees cry about what a great man Martin was.

Such bollocks.

He was a ruthless prick who treated everyone with the same amount of hate—myself included. Sure, he brought me to the States for holiday and part of summer break, but he only did that because he was forced to. He also insisted I call him *Martin* or *Father*, not *Dad*, because he wanted to ensure I wasn't confused since Mum was remarried. It was never a typical father-son relationship. He didn't teach me how to drive or throw a ball. The only thing he taught me was how to read stocks.

I really never liked him, and while his death was somewhat unexpected, it's been more of a burden than anything.

The only good thing to come out of this is that I now own one hundred percent of Dovetail Enterprises in both the States and

London. I can sell it off, keep it, grow it, or watch it burn to the ground.

However, the only thing I want to do is deal with Nicole.

She sits in the chair next to me, fidgeting with her papers. "First, I want to say I'm sorry for your loss."

"Don't be sorry. There's nothing sad about it."

Her lips part, and she nods. "Okay, I have a father, and I guess you could say I'd be like you are right now, but I'm still sorry."

"Is your father a selfish bastard who broke your mother's heart and then spoke ill of her constantly?"

I don't know why I'm asking her this, but I can't help but want to know more. Nicole has intrigued me from the moment I met her. Her little running away after dinner the other night only made me more curious.

"In fact, he is. My parents hate each other more than yours ever could of."

"Doubtful, but it seems we have quite a bit in common."

She smiles but drops her head in the way a teacher would when indulging a student but still on to their game. "Right."

"Anyway, I'm here in his place."

"So, do you want to postpone the meeting?" Nicole asks.

Absolutely not. I want to stay here, force her to be near me, find out what in the bloody hell caused her to rub my cock and then run away without a word. No, this meeting is happening now.

"That's not an option. I'm returning to London in a few days, and my schedule has no room for anything else. Unless, you're not ready . . ."

Nicole shifts in her seat. "I'm ready. Has the project changed?"

"Honestly, I don't know. Martin had a lot of deals on the table, so I'm gathering the information this week before I decide what stays and what goes. Why don't you tell me what you understood of this meeting."

She fills me in on what he explained. It's not a bad idea, and it's very similar to what I'm doing in London. Real estate space is limited for me, and to combat that, I'm going up with my buildings. I can sell hundreds of luxury units in a desirable area for a lot more money than building ten homes. It's rather interesting that my father was taking a similar approach here.

"I don't want to waste either of our time, Cal—" She catches herself. "Mr.?"

"Huxley."

"But you said . . ."

"I took my stepfather's last name. He was my dad in every way."

She gives a small smile. "I get it."

Feeling slightly uncomfortable, which is always what happens when I speak of my father, I shift the meeting back to the designs. "Show me another mock-up. I'd like to see what else you were thinking."

We go through the meeting, staying focused on her vision for the industrial-style condos. I'll admit, I'm much more traditional in my tastes for designs, but Nicole has a very good eye. Plus, she's American and knows what is selling here versus what is popular in England.

"Do you like this one?"

It's far more modern than I would've chosen. "It's a bit . . . stark."

She nods. "I can see that. It's really more masculine than I think would appeal to your average buyer. I have some others."

I try to keep my eyes from drifting to her face, but I can't seem to stop myself. She's truly one of the most beautiful women I've ever seen. Her eyes are a mix of blue and green, changing whenever the light hits them. Her golden hair is in loose curls, brushing over her tits. I can't even allow myself a moment of looking there or I'll never get through this meeting without my fucking cock standing straight up.

It's bad enough I'm semi-hard now.

"Do you like these better?" Nicole asks with her head tilted to the side.

"I like it very much."

Only I'm not talking about the drawings.

I like her, and even though we barely know anything about each other, I know that I want to find out everything there is. I've always believed that people who say they knew something was there the minute they met someone were lying. It's seemed quite ridiculous, but here I am, thinking the same way.

"Good. I can have—"

"You're hired," I say without thinking.

"What?"

There's no going back now. "You're hired."

She squints a little. "Yeah, I'm not sure this is going to be a good project for Dupree Designs."

"And why not?"

There is a lot of money in this project, as well as future condos I plan to put up if this goes well. For all the things Martin was, rash was not it. He must've smelled money to even take this meeting.

Nicole clears her throat and starts to put her papers in order. "You know, it's just never a good idea for people to get involved when there's some kind of . . . whatever between them."

"What is this whatever that's between us?"

She huffs. "This weirdness."

"There's nothing weird about what is going on here. I like you. I would've taken you back to my room, we would've fucked until the sun came up, and then we'd be sitting here now, talking about designs."

She laughs. "Yeah, that's where you're wrong. I wouldn't be

sitting here because I don't sleep with clients. Had I known you were my meeting today, there never would've been any flirting at the club."

"Then it's a good thing you chickened out," I tell her with a smirk.

"Excuse me?" She gets to her feet. "I didn't chicken out! I was in the bathroom, when I came out, you were gone."

She's bloody full of it. I saw her, and I know she saw me. Then she ran.

I lean back in my chair. "If that's what you believe is true, then who am I to argue?"

"That's right." She slaps the folder down. "You're no one to argue about that because I know what happened. You stand me up and then call me a chicken, please."

Absolutely adorable, that's what this woman is.

"So you mean, if you had known we were going to be sitting here today, you wouldn't have rubbed your hand on my cock and then ran off?"

Nicole's lips purse. "Maybe I realized your cock wasn't worth touching again. If it was a bit bigger . . ."

I chuckle. This girl is unlike anyone else I've ever met. Most women would be horrified at the insinuation, but she actually insulted me back. "We both know my cock is plenty big enough, darling. I saw your eyes widen . . . and that was just a semi."

Her lips part, and I see her breath catch. "Wow, conceited much?"

"Not at all. I just know you're lying about the other night, to me and yourself. I saw the way you were looking at me all night."

"Like you're a pompous asshole?"

I rise, move closer to her, and run my finger from her shoulder to her wrist. "No, like you wanted to know what it felt like to be beneath me all night, and believe me, I wanted to know the same thing."

Her eyes flame with passion. I can feel her pulse race beneath my fingertips. The room feels smaller, and then she shakes her head and gets to her feet. "And this, Mr. Huxley, is why Dupree Designs can't work with you."

"So, does that mean you intend to sleep with me?"

She pulls her hand back and glares. "Not even remotely a possibility."

I smile and nod. "Good, then you'll start Monday on my project."

I had planned to finish here, toss my father's plans out, and get back home, but this is much more interesting.

Maybe spending some time in the States is exactly what I need . . .

seven

. . .

Nicole

WHY DOES this man make my blood boil and not in the I'm-so-pissed-off-I-want-to-punch-you kind of way? Why can't I hate him and not want to strip him and screw him until he can't walk again?

It has to be the accent. That's all.

"Listen," I say as I push myself back into professional, business-owner mode. "I'm very sorry for what I just said. I know whatever happened at the club probably upset you, but this company means everything to me, and I work really hard to continue to grow it. I only have one rule in life: do not mix business with pleasure."

Callum exhales and moves back a little. "It's a very good rule to follow."

Oh, that was easier than I thought it would be.

"Thank you."

"Since we haven't mixed anything, you should have no problem taking this job then," he states.

"Well . . ."

"Your one rule hasn't been broken," Callum reminds me.

"Yes, but . . ."

"And my father's notes were clear that you were relentless in pursuing him."

I try to talk again. "Not exactly how that happened—"

"That you called and called to get this meeting, and you were willing to meet him anywhere to prove your designs were superior."

Jesus. Who takes notes like that? Yes, I was a bit pushy, but it's because these condos are perfect and the exact style I would fit into. It was for his own good as well.

"Okay, but what I'm saying is—"

Callum cuts me off again. "That you want the job."

Okay, this guy is pissing me off now. "Mr. Huxley, please allow me to finish my sentence this time." He moves his hand over his lips like a zipper, and I almost roll my eyes at how cute he looks. That is exactly why I have to walk away from this. I'll sell my body before I put myself in a bad situation with a man again, especially one capable of completely wrecking me. "Thank you. I wanted this job before, but as I said, my business is a little overwhelmed right now, and I can't possibly take on a project this large."

I said it, and I won't take it back even though I'm pretty sure I don't have to sell my body because I just fucked myself over pretty well.

He stays still, hand over those full lips I want to smash mine against, and doesn't speak.

I wait.

And wait some more.

Until he finally moves. "I see."

"You do?"

"Yes." Callum nods. "You need more money. I haven't made this enticing enough for you."

"Umm, what?"

That wasn't what I said. It's nothing remotely close to the words that came out of my mouth.

"Your original bid was definitely low, which leads me to think it was to get the old man here. Then, once you proved you were worth his time, you planned to get him up to a reasonable design fee." Callum begins to pace. "Brilliant really. I, on the other hand, don't have time to play hardball, Nicole. I'd much rather we just be honest with one another. So, give me what your new bid would be."

I've never had a client push to work with me this hard. It doesn't make sense. Fine. I'll go ridiculously high, a number that no one in their right mind would ever take, and then we can be done.

"You won't like the number I come up with," I tell him with defiance.

"Try me."

"A million dollars." I toss the number out, knowing there is not a chance in hell we'll come close to that.

"You're right." Callum sighs. "That number isn't what I had in mind."

Oh, thank God. Now I can berate myself while I'm moving into a cardboard box, or worse . . . into my mother's house.

"That's what I feel I'm worth. I'm very sorry."

Really, I should be apologizing to myself. Sometimes being stubborn—which I'm being at this moment— is a curse. I'm a total idiot, not at all acting in the best interests of my company. I'm being a dumbass and walking away from a job because this stupid man scares me.

He's just like Andy.

God, just thinking his name makes me want to fall to the floor and cry.

I don't fucking cry.

Crying makes you weak, and I'm not now nor will I ever be again.

His smile does things to my stomach. The way his eyes crinkle in the corner when he's thinking—like right now.

"You lowballed me again," Callum comes back. "That's why it's not what I had in mind."

Lowballed him? Is he drunk? That wasn't a lowball bid. There is no way anyone in their right mind would take that.

"What?"

"I'm not a man who enjoys games." He moves closer. "I prefer you come in with your best offer instead of the back and forth, don't you?" Callum doesn't give me time to answer. He just starts speaking again. "I think it's important for businesses to have a sort of trust. If you come in low, and I accept, it creates this animosity, as though your work isn't valued. I much prefer we never have that issue, especially since it's clear we both have rather strong feelings for each other. So, I'll write down the number, and then I'll see you on Monday."

I'm starting to wonder if he's hard of hearing. I am not going to take the damn job, so Monday isn't happening. And I refuse to let myself have feelings for him, which is why I'm walking away.

"Mr. Huxley—"

"Callum. I believe we've both earned the right to first names since you've had your hand on my cock already, wouldn't you agree?"

"Sure, but you're not hearing me," I explain.

Without responding, he begins to write something on a piece of paper. What is wrong with men? Do they think this crazy dominant behavior is attractive? I mean . . . it kind of is, but still.

"I heard every word. I just don't accept your terms," he says, and then he hands me the folded piece of paper, touches my cheek, and walks out of the room.

Because I have no idea what the hell happened, I flop down into the seat and unfold the paper.

When I see the number written, I almost fall out of my chair. This man is going to get exactly what he wants.

"*Three* million dollars!" Kristin screams and then throws a pillow at me. "Are you kidding?"

I drain another glass of wine and fill that baby right back up. "No, I'm not kidding. What the hell do I do?"

"You take that money and design him the best apartments that Tampa has ever seen!"

Why did it have to be him? Why couldn't he go back to London so I could just get on with my life? It's been a week since I had sex. A week! That doesn't happen for me. I like sex. No, scratch that, I love it, and since I met Callum, I can't even bring myself to call one of my hookups.

He's broken me.

The stupid asshole broke my vagina without even touching it.

"You don't get it," I tell Kris.

"Clearly, I don't."

Might as well tell her everything. "He's the guy I ran away from."

She puts her glass down and stares at me. "You mean the one you Heathergated from?"

I nod.

"Well, that explains why you're not dancing around and you're acting like three *million* dollars is a bad thing." Kristin leans back.

"Let's be honest for one second here." I sigh. "I'm good at my job, but I'm not worth three million dollars. This is some sort of trap."

"Maybe the job is worth that," she suggests.

"It's a lot of work. I mean, a lot. He wants fifteen different designs and for me to oversee every detail in each unit while they're being built. They're completely customizable, and he wants to make sure that I'm involved at all levels. I'll basically be designing each loft for each client. I won't have time for any other jobs, but I don't make three million dollars! I wonder if this is a sex trap . . ."

"Yeah, it's totally a sexy trap," she says sarcastically.

"Well, there's no other explanation!"

It doesn't make sense. If I were any other designer, would he pay that?

No. No, he wouldn't.

"Okay, let's go back because I feel like I'm missing something here." Kristin scoots forward. "What happened that night that you're not telling me?"

The best part about my three best friends is that they each fill a void. I think we do the same across the board for each other. Kristin and I never really were close as kids, it wasn't until she found me, on the floor, desperate to stop the pain that we started to lean on each other. She came to the house the night I lost the only man I've ever loved. It wasn't pretty but she didn't judge me or make me feel worse about my life. She held my hand through the aftermath. In all the years before that, she'd never seen me cry.

I'm pretty sure she was terrified.

"He reminds me of Andy. He's sexy, smooth, funny, and the only difference is that he has a British accent that makes me want to do unspeakable things. I craved being near him. It was like my body was being pulled toward his and I couldn't stop it. He looked at me as though he couldn't make himself stop either. It was exactly like that for me before, and look how that worked out."

Kristin shakes her head. "Andy was a prick. He hurt you because he was a liar."

"I trusted myself!"

"Okay, but that doesn't mean you're going to be wrong again." She tries to comfort me. She sucks at comforting people. "You're working for this guy, not falling in love with him, right?"

"Yes."

At least that's the plan.

"But you're scared?" she asks.

I don't get scared of men. I get angry or turned on, but scared isn't really my thing. I'm confident, and when I set my mind to something, I accomplish it. What scares me is that I was running away at the club when I should have been marching right past him, getting into my car, and driving off. That is what has me shitting myself.

"I don't want to get involved," I tell her.

"Then don't."

"I didn't plan to get involved with Andy."

Kristin leans back. "I get that, but you had no idea he was married, Nicole. He lied to you, led you on, and made you think you were designing a life together and not just his office. Also, it's really not fair to use a relationship from fifteen years ago as your benchmark for all men."

"Whatever."

Kristin huffs. "You're ridiculous."

"Maybe I am."

"You know, not every guy is the same . . ."

The thing is, I thought there was something wrong about four months in. He never wanted to meet my friends, family, or even let me tell people about us. I had to keep our relationship a secret, sneak around because he was an important businessman and being single was part of his sales pitch. At the time, I accepted it because it sounded somewhat plausible. The longer the relationship carried on, the less those excuses made sense. I couldn't explain it, but my intuition was firing off at every turn.

He was too perfect. Everything always worked out exactly the way it should, and it made me wary of our relationship. I didn't know he was married and his wife was expecting until the very end. But if I'd trusted my gut, I would've dug deeper and saved myself a lot of heartache.

It took me a long time to see my failure, to really explore my fears, because I already knew the answer—I didn't want to know the truth.

"Well, I was really wrong back then . . ."

She sighs. "Yes, but that doesn't mean you're wrong *now*. You're not the same girl anymore. You were young, and he took advantage of you."

"Being young isn't an excuse. I'm at fault here. I should've pushed for answers. I wasn't young—I was dumb."

"So a man, who was ten years older than you, tells you everything you want to hear and gives you a dream opportunity that will set you up financially and career wise, plays on your emotions, gets you to trust him, and then fucks your head up is okay?"

Of course, it's not okay. I never said I wasn't victimized, but she's missing the point. "I played a role in this, Kris. Your husband fucked around on you, did you not blame her?"

She shakes her head. "This isn't even remotely the same. Jillian knew that Scott was married and had two kids. She was an active participant in that affair. Hell, she set up their little sex weekend trips, called me to tell me he was out of town, and then hopped on a flight. She tried to be my friend, and all the while, she was screwing my husband. You left him the minute you found out."

"We're going to have to agree to disagree," I tell her as I drop my head back against the couch.

I loved Andy more than anything. Yeah, I was twenty-three and naïve, but I was smart enough to know better. Too often, we blame things on being too young to understand, but that doesn't mean that Andy's wife wasn't devastated. She had to find out that some blonde with big tits was fucking her husband. He was going to leave her, and I was why.

Me.

I was the homewrecker, and I've hated myself ever since.

"I'm going to ask you something . . ." Kristin warns.

"Aren't you supposed to ask someone if you can ask a question, not tell them you're going to? "

"Sure, if I gave a shit about your boundaries."

I roll my eyes. "Nice."

"Oh, please!" She laughs. "You are the last one to talk. Anyway, my question is this: do you think you deserve love and happiness? I'm not saying with your friends or work, but a real relationship. A man who will love you, honor you, and give you a life built on trust?"

I don't answer her. Not because I don't know what my response would be but because it will launch us into another three-hour fight that I don't have the energy for. I don't know what I deserve, but sometimes, I wonder if never finding a man who is worthy is part of my punishment.

Instead, I release a deep breath and smile. "I think I have the life I want, and for now, that's all I need."

Kristin's eyes narrow, probably knowing there's some hidden meaning in my words. "Well, I think you're wrong, Nicole. I think you want more, you just don't want to. To answer my own question, though, there is no one in this world who deserves to be loved more than you, my beautiful friend. No one."

If only I believed her, maybe I could forgive myself and learn to let someone in.

eight

· · ·

Nicole

OKAY, *stay calm, he's just a man.*

A sexy, tall, beautiful man with a voice that does strange things to my lady bits, but whatever.

This is business. It's a simple transaction between Dovetail Enterprises and Dupree Designs. It means no sex, no flirting, no dreaming of ripping off his clothes and riding his cock like a cowgirl on her stud. All of that want and those ideas were pre-contract.

I have three million reasons to make this work.

"Nicole, Mr. Huxley is here," Kim says through the intercom.

"Please send him in."

I manage to get the words out without sounding completely breathless. I'm taking that as progress.

I stand because sitting feels like giving him the upper hand and I need all the power I can grab before Callum walks in and steals it all for himself. His presence is like catnip to girls like me. I don't really think I have "daddy issues," per se. It's more like powerful men make me feel good. When my father walked into a room, people noticed. There was something alluring about that.

Watching other people stop and stare, wondering, wanting, and attaining.

A few seconds later, Callum enters. My heart begins to race as I take him in. His broad shoulders, deep-blue eyes, and sandy-brown hair are even sexier than I remember. And his watch. God, his fucking watch. How does a man make a watch look that good? He touches it as though he could read my mind, adjusting the face, the very big face that still looks somewhat small on his arm. How the hell that's possible, I'll never know, but it hasn't stopped me from trying to figure it out. All I've done the last three days is dream of him.

In very naughty ways.

Now he's in front of me, and I'm suddenly very warm.

"Nicole," he says with warmth as he moves forward.

"Callum." I clear my throat and then walk toward him. "It's great to see you."

His eyes glimmer in the sunlight, and when we're close, I extend my hand. He takes it, and then pulls me closer and places a kiss on my cheek, which isn't at all what I expect.

I'm so thrown off that I don't prepare myself not to inhale his cologne. I don't think to guard myself so I won't practically collide against his solid chest. No, I go face first, nearly toppling over in my four-inch heels.

His arms wrap around me, stopping me from going down.

I forget, because I'm just a girl, that I shouldn't look up at him. I shouldn't stand here, in his arms, breathing in the musky scent that surrounds him, but here I am, doing just that.

"Are you all right?"

The sound of his voice snaps me out of my daze. "Yes, thank you." I push off his chest and right myself. "Sorry, I wasn't expecting that."

He grins. "I guess we both have been thrown off a bit by the recent events."

You can say that again.

"Well, I appreciate you taking the meeting today. I know you're heading back to London soon."

He nods. "Yes, I'm due to leave first thing tomorrow, but I may be delayed another two days. I haven't decided yet."

The ocean that would be between us is one of the reasons I agreed to this deal. Since it's kind of hard to fuck someone when they aren't on the same continent, I would have been safe.

"After a lot of consideration, I'd like to take on the project. I think that with my designs and the plans your father had in place, we will work really well together. Hopefully, there will be a lot of great opportunities for collaboration in the future."

Kristin had brought up a lot of great points regarding the difference with Andy and Callum, but the most important one had been me. I'm in control here. My heart is in no danger unless I allow it to be. At the end of the day, business is business, and I would hate myself for walking away because of some guy I don't even know.

So, for the sake of the company I've spent my life building, I'm not passing this up. I have a renewed sense of determination. A level-head. And no way will I end up horizontal with Callum. Vertical is the only option.

But there's always wall sex.

No. Not even going there.

Callum smirks at me as though he can read my mind. "I'm glad you've come around to me."

"Regarding the project." I clear up any confusion on what I'm agreeing to.

He shrugs. "For now."

"Forever."

"I'd like to discuss the details a little deeper," Callum says as he sits.

I take my own seat, thankful that my desk is oversized so it puts additional space between us. "Okay."

"Over dinner."

Well, should've seen that one coming. "Why not discuss it now?"

Callum leans back, cracking his neck while his eyes stay glued on me. "Because I don't really know many people here other than Ted, and we both know he's a tool."

I let out a short laugh. "And smells like onions."

"That too," Callum agrees. "That said, I'd like to have a dinner meeting, go over the details, and get some things on paper. I'm assuming you *do* entertain clients from time to time?"

"I do." This is such a bad idea, but again, I'm going to treat this like I would any other client I would have. Reality is that he's paying me a fuckton of money, if he wants dinner, then I need to find a way to make it through without taking my panties off. "Dinner tonight would be possible. Unfortunately, I'm babysitting my niece tomorrow so it's my only availability."

He smiles. "Tonight would be fine. I would like to head back to London knowing we're at least on the right track."

"I agree."

"You have no other clients you need to work with?"

I have other small projects, but he doesn't need to know that. "I'm committed to this project, Callum. I assure you that I can handle it."

His fingers are steepled in front of him, and he nods. "That's good to know. Considering the rather large sum of money, I'm just ensuring your time is open."

"We're fine."

"You know, part of what makes me a good businessman is being able to read people. I had a feeling about you the minute we met. I understand now what my father saw in you because I see it as well." His voice is deep and raspy. "I believe this is a great beginning for us."

The compliment washes over me. "I won't let you or your late father down."

Callum gets to his feet. "I didn't think you would."

I come around the desk, and his hand touches the small of my back as we get to my door. It's a gesture many men make, but there's something about his touch that feels different. I shove it down, focusing on not falling into his arms again. "Thank you. I'll have my secretary send you the details for dinner tonight."

He grins. "I look forward to it."

Just like earlier, he leans forward, only this time I'm a little more prepared. His lips touch my cheek, staying a second past what is considered friendly, his nose grazes the skin, and I swear my legs go weak, but I stay upright.

I swallow down the desire to wrap my arms around him and kiss the fuck out of him. "Tonight, then."

His voice is huskier than a moment ago. "Tonight."

He leaves the room, and I flop down onto the couch with my arm over my face. I am in so much freaking trouble.

―――――――――――――

"What are you wearing to this dinner?" Heather asks on the video call.

"A muumuu?" I huff and then toss another shirt onto the bed.

"Like you would even own one of those!"

"Shut up."

She laughs and then points. "Oh, wear the red dress!"

"I want him *not to* want to have sex with me, Heather! Not fuck my brains out against the car."

Seriously, how is she helping? This is what happens when your best friend runs off to watch her husband film another movie. I'm happy for Eli, but does she *have* to go with him all the damn time? Doesn't he know she has friends who are needy as fuck and require her attention? Selfish husbands, all of them.

"Good luck with that. I'm straight and I'd do you."

"Awww." I smile into the camera. "I love when you talk dirty to me. But you're a prude, so you'd never actually follow through. I, on the other hand, would at least make out with you. I'm more into two men, but I could make an exception if you're really interested."

She laughs. "Nope, I'm good."

"You sure?"

Heather shakes her head.

"I'm just saying I would help you out."

"That's because you're a freak."

I grin. "Amen."

It isn't as if I'm ashamed of it. I like sex. Nothing wrong with it. I'm safe, always sure of my surroundings, and I know my limits.

"Speaking of, any new trysts you've been holding out on."

I grab the phone, flop back onto my bed, and frown. "Nope. Since meeting Mr. Fuck-Me-With-An-Accent, I haven't. I think I'm sick, you know? Like one of those illnesses that makes your vag dry up. I think it's terminal."

"Death by lack of sex?"

"Yes! That's what this is. I need a good fuck so I can stop thinking about him and his dick."

Heather rolls her eyes. "I'm pretty sure that won't work."

"Pretty sure and sure are two different things," I inform her.

Do I think it'll work? Nope. I'm *pretty sure* I'll be dreaming of Callum's cock until I experience it, which means I'll be dreaming about it forever.

Why is it that when you know you can't have something, you want it more? It isn't fair that now he's my client. I should have slept with him at the club. Then I wouldn't be imagining what it would be like. Maybe he would've been horrible. Then I could be all, *no thanks, rode the ride and never want to again* instead of standing in line, hoping the line moves.

"Well, you can't do it, and you know why."

Once again, she's super helpful. "I'm aware of this."

"Although . . ." Heather sighs. "You made this silly rule. It's not like you can't break it."

"I have my reasons."

Heather knows of Andy and the very basics of what happened. She doesn't know he was married or that I was a week away from buying a home for him and myself. She doesn't know that I found out I was pregnant a week before I found out about his wife. She doesn't know that I lost that baby or that Andy told me he was going to work things out with her because it was the "right thing."

My friends would never judge me. I know they would see him as the villain in that story, but the truth is, it's me who judges me. I was the reason that girl had to wonder where he was at night. I was making love to a man who didn't belong to me.

When I found out I was pregnant, I wanted to die.

I was horrified when I found out that his wife was also pregnant.

I was distraught to think he was sleeping with both of us.

I was terrified that my entire livelihood would be affected because of one man.

It's not a silly rule to me.

It's the only way to survive.

"Okay, whatever. I'm not saying it's a good idea to sleep with your clients on a normal basis, but clearly, there's something here, no?"

"All that's clear is the contract for three million reasons not to fuck him. So, I'm going to keep that in sight, dress like a nun, try to tone down my hotness—as if that's even possible—and make it through dinner without touching his junk again."

"Again?" she yells and almost drops the phone. "Wait, again?"

I groan. Me and my big mouth. "Yes, I touched him once already. At the club, I was being . . . me . . . and I grazed it, rubbed it a little."

"Seriously, I don't understand you. You met the guy once and you managed to grab his dick?"

"She did what?" I hear Eli in the background.

Yes, let's let him weigh in too . . .

"I touched the man's dick, Eli. I was sitting next to him and he smelled good, so I ran my hand over it. Then I ran out like Heather did after she fucked you the first time. Happy? I'm as big of an ass as she is," I announce.

He comes into the camera's view. "I bet he really likes you now." Eli chuckles.

"Why? Because I'm an ass?"

"No." He shakes his head. "You're a tease. There's nothing a guy likes more than a challenge. You threw down the gauntlet, be ready for the games, sweetheart."

"What is wrong with your entire sex? Are you all morons?" I ask rhetorically.

"Pretty much."

Heather shakes her head with a smile.

"Fifty bucks says you end up on your back tonight," he challenges.

I narrow my eyes at him. "I should've been a man, Eli Walsh, because I, too, like a challenge. I'm about to have fifty bucks and watch you lose to a girl. Game on."

This is going to be like taking candy from a baby.

nine

· · ·

Callum

"HANDLE IT, MILO," I groan into the receiver at my brother. There are two projects in London that require special attention. My brother, who is supposed to be my right-hand man and handling them for me—isn't. Instead, he has decided he needed a holiday because the new model he's dating wanted to go on a trip.

I'm going to kill the wanker.

"I'm doing my best. You went away at a shit time," he says, and I hear the woman giggle in the background.

I've had it with him. I get that he's pissed at me for whatever bullshit reason, but this is ridiculous. I don't know how I'm supposed to trust him to get things done when he's taking off at whatever whim he has.

"No, my father died. I had no damn choice. You want to have more responsibility at the company, then earn it!" I yell and then hang up the line.

I close my eyes, rubbing my temples before I need to go be charming to Nicole. I don't know what my goal is other than be around her for a bit longer. There's no real work-related conversation we need to have—I just need to have her.

I'm still rubbing my temples when my phone rings again, and I don't pause before accepting the call.

"Hello, Cal." My mum's warm voice makes me feel better.

I don't know what it is about my mum, but just the sound of her voice allows me to calm down. She's always been this way, and I'd like to think my personality comes from her. I can't remember a time when she was cross and lost her temper. It was always her who kept her head about her during times when Milo and I were acting up.

"Hello, Mum."

"How is America?" There's no mistaking the disdain in her voice. My mum loved America once. She would've moved across the pond in a heartbeat, but my father alone solidified the reason she'll never come here again, not even now that he's dead.

"It's bloody hot. I'll be returning home in a few days."

"What's the delay?" she asks.

A beautiful blonde who has captured my heart. However, I don't say that because she'll scold me relentlessly. Mum isn't a fan of any kind of romance with an American. She learned that lesson. "Just tying up a few loose ends. Now that I have full control of the American company, I need to ensure things are in order so I'm not flying back and forth."

She's quiet for a few moments. "And have you handled things with your father's estate?"

"Yes. He's all settled now."

Meaning—buried.

"Well, I'm sure you did a nice job for him, even if he didn't do much for you."

He didn't, but I won't agree with her or defend him. He doesn't deserve either, and she really won't listen anyway.

"I'm sorry," I tell her.

"Don't be. I had a wonderful husband. Your dad was a wonderful man."

"Yes, he was."

I had a father and a dad. I was fortunate to have Milo's father as my stepfather growing up. He never treated me different. He loved me as though I was his biological son and was always there no matter what.

My father was a check each month and obligatory visits. Most of the time, I followed him around like a puppy, learning how to be a businessman.

"I have to run, but I'll ring you before I head back."

"Okay, darling. You be careful over there. Don't fall in love and not come home, promise?"

"I won't, Mum," I say with a laugh.

She didn't say anything about having some fun though . . .

"Right this way." The hostess escorts Nicole and me to a table in the back.

God, she's fucking gorgeous.

That's all I can think as she walks in front of me. She's wearing a deep-purple dress that cuts off at her knees. I don't know if she's trying not to be sexy, but there's not a chance in hell she's not.

Her hair is in a loose ponytail with strands falling around her face. Her eyes are simple in makeup, but that only allows me to see her light blue eyes even better. She's breathtaking.

We get to the table, and she sits straight in her chair. "This place is okay?"

I nod. "It's great."

She smiles, and I want to ensure that stays there all night. "Do you come here often?"

"Not really. I'm usually working late and this place is always packed, but my best friend's husband knows the owner."

"That must be a nice perk?"

Nicole tilts her head back and forth. "Well, I don't usually ask Eli to pull strings, but I thought this would be a great place for our dinner."

I smirk and lean back. "You wanted to impress me?"

"I wanted to make sure you saw that I'm *professional* and value the *business* relationship we have established." Nicole grabs her glass of water and sips.

Instead of jumping in immediately, I let her wait a bit. No matter what she says, there's something between us. We both know it, and it is only getting stronger. The more I'm around her, the more I want to stay close.

Once she places the glass down, I move my hand. "Business partners can be friends."

"Sure, but we're not talking about us."

"Aren't we?"

She sighs. "Callum, please don't make this hard. I want to work with you. I would love to be friends with you, but we can't go further than that, okay?"

I showed my hand too soon. Now I have to back up. I raise my hands in the air with a smile. "Truce?"

Nicole's red lips turn up into a smile. "Truce."

"I promise I won't say another inappropriate word. If I do, you can throw the water from your glass in my face. It's a bit dramatic, but I'm sure it will make you smile."

"I would never. Well, I totally would, but not until you've seen the designs and sent me half the money." She laughs as if she's joking, though, I'm not sure she is.

"Then I guess we shouldn't chance it," I say as the waiter walks over.

Nicole and I order a bottle of wine, a few starters, and our dinners. I love that she isn't afraid to eat. She gets a steak instead of the rabbit food most women order at restaurants. Lord knows my ex did. She felt eating in front of me was going to make her less attractive. Eight years later, I learned it was her personality that was ugly.

"So, have you always had a stake in Dovetail?" Nicole asks as she runs her finger along the rim of her wine glass.

"In a way. My father was only generous after he realized I wasn't an idiot. After seeing I was rather savvy when it came to business, he gave me a bigger role. Then he decided he wanted a London office, so we built one."

"Wow." She sits back in her seat. "That's impressive."

"Yes, well, I wanted to make my own name in the UK, so I put up most of the startup money, the rest was an investment from my father. He was a silent partner, and after the first year of being profitable, I bought him out completely."

His name had no weight over there, and my surname, Huxley, did. Martin provided the funds to help with the startup because I agreed to use Dovetail as the company name. It was purely a financial transaction for me, regardless of him believing it was something to pay tribute to him.

He was an arrogant bastard. He absolutely hated that I took Huxley as my name when I was a boy. I was eight, and I wanted to be like my stepfather, so I asked my mum, and she somehow convinced Martin.

"I understand, probably more than you would think," Nicole says with a sigh.

"Really?"

She nods. "My father is a big deal around here. He's loaded and married to a girl about my age. You know . . . the typical old-man-with-money type. He offered to basically pay for my entire business if it meant he could profit off it, but I said no. I built Dupree Designs completely alone."

"And now it's my turn to be impressed."

"Hardly. You're much more successful than I am."

I don't see it that way. She had to work harder than I did. "I

had a lot of doors open for me. My brother and I worked tire-
lessly in the beginning to establish ourselves. Honestly, we got
lucky most of the time."

"How so?" she asks.

"Milo found a piece of property that seemed too good to be
true. He and I took what little money we had and took a gamble.
Thankfully, it paid off. We made a lot of money off that land.
Enough to buy my father out and establish ourselves as a premier
real estate investment company in London."

"And now you're here . . ." she says with a smile.

"Here we are . . ."

Her blue eyes are soft as she looks at me. "I guess we are."

Something stirs deep in my gut, making me want her more
than I did before. She looks unguarded and even more beautiful, if
that's possible. I want to touch her and feel her soft skin beneath
mine, but I can't.

I lift my glass, and she does the same. Keeping my promise
tonight is going to be very difficult.

ten

. . .

Nicole

I'M TOTALLY NOT DOING WELL at this whole not stripping him in my mind game. Since he picked me up, I've thought of about thirty different ways I could have sex with him. It isn't fair that the one man I seem to want is the one man I can't have.

Stupid sex rules.

"Tell me about your brother," I say and then take a bite of my steak.

"He's a fucking moron."

"Well, don't hold back."

Callum grins. "Sorry, I had a bit of a fight with him before dinner. He's brilliant when he wants to work, which seems to be very little lately. We grew up in the same house, but lived very different lives. I hoped he would've changed this last year when I promoted him, but it seemed to only make him more of a bloody fool."

I could listen to him talk all day. His voice is this extra layer of yumminess that I want to swim in all day. The words just sound sexier with the accent.

Eli was right, I'm totally going to end up fucking his brains out tonight while he's talking dirty to me. I'm not sure if I'll be on top or he will, but it'll be damn good either way. I already know he's packing a rather large pistol in those pants. I can't wait to cock that gun and watch it go off.

"Nicole?" Callum's voice snaps me out of my little fantasy.

"Hmm?"

Callum smiles. "Am I interrupting something?"

Shit.

I was totally busted having a really good daydream, but I remember my rule.

No sex. No flirting. No life-altering sex with the Brit.

"Nope. Sorry, just envisioning a design." Lie. Lie. Lie.

"A design?"

Sex is sort of like a design. I mean . . . I thought about the bed. It counts.

"Yup. For the lofts. I was thinking about color and surfaces." Hard, cold, granite that my back will lie on while his hot, hard body is—

"For the lofts?"

He's totally not buying it, but I'm going to sell this. I have no other choice. "Yes, I was wondering if I should go more glam or maybe industrial. I'm not sure. Maybe those can be the two options. We could do a more high-end modern feel and then a more warehouse type option for those who want that look. It might be great."

Please believe me. Please believe me.

"Those are both good options." Callum's voice is filled with disbelief. "If that was what you were thinking."

"You never know when inspiration will strike. It's the craziest thing that us creative types deal with. I think I have some great ideas that I'll be able to show you soon."

Callum swipes his mouth and then places his napkin on the

table. "All right. Since we're talking business, I'd like to discuss some of the finer points before we sign the contract."

I knew this was coming since it was the entire purpose of this dinner. I need the contract signed, until then, I need to reel myself in. "Sure, let's do that."

I reach into my purse and pull out the piece of paper and pen I shoved in there.

He smiles, and I preen under his silent praise. "Impressive."

"What is?"

"You come prepared."

"Oh, I always come," I say, pause, and then mentally slap myself, "prepared! I always come prepared, that is."

Callum's eyes deepen, and I don't have a single doubt that his thoughts went exactly where mine did. Coming in the most glorious way—together. Jesus, this is out of hand. I need to get a grip.

His lips turn up into a smirk. Most girls would get embarrassed, but I don't. I smirk right back at him. While this might be bordering on flirting, I don't have a rule against flirting.

"I like to make sure the people I come with," Callum's voice drops lower, "are always satisfied."

"Good to know. I'm sure they're all very happy," I say and then lean back, putting us firmly back in the friends and business associates zone.

He hesitates for a second before he concedes. "How about we make you happy, let's work out the deal."

Business always makes me happy.

We go back and forth for the next twenty minutes, negotiating all the details, trying to find a middle ground. I'd like to consider myself a very intelligent businesswoman. There's an art to negotiations, and my father is the Michelangelo of this world. He can make men bend to his will, and I've watched and learned.

Callum, however, seems to have been his apprentice. I don't

know how we got so turned around at one point, but I'm pretty sure I went off the rails, which never happens.

I try to circle back around. "Okay, but you want me to design the lofts *here* in the States."

"Yes."

"Right. So why would I need to come to London?"

"Because that's where I will be. There will be meetings I'd like you to attend."

Makes sense, but I don't like this. "This is what they make video conferencing for. I'll need to be here, watching over the entire project. When the general contractor goes away, bad things happen."

I've been down this road too many times. You head out of town, think everything is fine, and come back to chaos. I have a lot riding on this thing, so I'm not going to fuck it up.

"Yes, but you're not the GC."

"No, but I'm going to watch that man like a hawk," I explain.

Callum grins. "Hmm, maybe I should be the GC then."

"Cute."

"I'd rather think I am."

I roll my eyes. "I didn't say you were cute. I said your little play there was cute."

He leans in. "It's the same thing to me."

If he could just have a flaw somewhere, that would be awesome. Then I could pick at it like a scab until it bleeds and maybe becomes infected. Then I really wouldn't want to touch it.

"All right, let's finish this so we can both sign on the dotted line. Is there anything else that you'd like to work into the contract?" I ask.

"Yes."

"What would that be?"

He smiles. "You."

"Me?"

Callum doesn't budge. His eyes stay on mine, showing me no mercy as I try to dig for a deeper meaning.

"Yes, I want you to be available to me for other projects I have in mind. This isn't the only building I'll be putting up in the area. I'd like to have a designer on staff."

Okay, so not where my dirty mind went. I clasp my hands in front of me, giving myself a beat. I'm not sure how to respond, and I need to be smart and not reactive. He's basically telling me that he'd like to work with me in the future, which bodes well for my company. Callum is now running his father's company, which means connections as well. That said, I'm not willing to walk away from *my* company to work for his.

"Can you clarify exactly what that looks like for you?"

His eyes deepen and then turn back. "It means you'd work for me."

"That's not going to work for me," I say, giving him a slight shake of my head.

"Why not?"

"Because I own my company, Mr. Huxley."

"Callum," he corrects.

"Right. Well, I don't want to work for anyone," I tell him without room for negotiation. Then I hear my father's voice in the back of my mind: *There's always room for negotiation. You only have to know what you're negotiating.*

He nods. "It's something I'd like to bring in-house."

I'd like to bring you in my house, too, but we don't always get what we want.

"I understand, and if that's the case, then I'm not the right designer for you. I'm sorry, but that's not an option."

I really hope I'm not fucking this up. This is a lot of money, and I just basically went all in on a shitty hand.

Callum studies me, watching for something that he'll never see. I have weaknesses, but I don't show them. No matter how deep he looks, he'll never see the timid girl who wanted her daddy to love her more than his job. He'll never know the girl who broke down so bad she couldn't get out of bed. Who lied to her friends because a man destroyed her. He will never know the depths of pain I felt when I realized I wasn't as strong as I thought.

I was Nicole Dupree, the woman who would never let a man be the cause of anguish ever again.

I was the badass who broke hearts, not had hers broken.

"I'm sorry to hear that."

Shit. I really need this job. I just can't let him know that. Not because I need money, I'm fine there, but because this is the next level. This is where I go from decorating for housewives who want a fresher look to contracts that will have me set for life.

I'm about to speak when the waiter comes over with the check. I go to grab for it, but Callum is quicker. "Never going to happen when we're at dinner."

"This is a business meeting," I clarify.

Callum's eyes meet mine, and he's clearly irritated by that. "We're eating because I asked to have the meeting over dinner, are we not?"

"Yes."

"Then it's dinner and a meeting that I initiated."

My defiant side wants to tell him it's also a business meeting, but I choose not to. I have a feeling there's a deeper fight.

"Fine, still doesn't change the fact that we're at an impasse."

He rubs the scruff on his chin, looking off, and I shift in my seat. Everything he does is sexy. It really isn't fair.

"What about coming on as a contract base? You would be a sub-employee, but still remain as your own boss. However, you must fulfill your contract with Dovetail," he says, causing me to jump a little.

Damn it. That would work. I could sever the agreement if I build in enough clauses, but it could also give me the leverage I need going forward. I could work with Callum and still maintain Dupree Designs. Also, contracts can be broken if both parties have issues. It's honestly the perfect option. However, if I agree immediately, he'll have some power over me, which is definitely something I can't allow.

I have a feeling that Callum would feast on it.

There's something else I'd much rather him feast on.

"I'll think about it. I need to look over my schedule before I can commit."

He smiles as though I just played right into his hand. "I'll expect an answer by tomorrow."

Seems I gave him something after all.

"You should buy this dress," my mother says as she holds up the most hideous thing I've ever seen. "It would look fantastic on you."

"The only way you're getting me into that is if you're burying me, even then, I'd haunt you for it."

She rolls her eyes. "You're so dramatic."

For a woman who taught me most of what I know regarding decorating, she has the worst taste when it comes to clothes. It's truly baffling. Her home is straight out of a magazine. The finest draperies, linens, stone, cabinets, and anything else she can spend my father's fortune on, but clothes? It's as if she's clueless.

Her wardrobe consists of pants suits and dresses that make the nuns look like they're in bikinis.

"Mom, please, try this on. I swear you'll look great." I lift a dress that is so small not even I would wear it.

"Nicole! That is highly inappropriate."

Yes. Yes, it is. "That's the point. You give me clothes I hate, and I'm showing you the same. Seriously, look at that thing you're holding, would I ever put that on?"

She sighs and puts it back onto the rack. "I do wish you'd dressed a little more demurely."

"Why? I'm young."

"Not *that* young."

Whatever. Arguing with her about this is pointless. Usually, I do it because it's fun, but today, I feel out of sorts. Last night took a lot out of me. I barely slept after my dinner with Callum. I kept thinking about him. How he looked at me. How it was as if he could see through to my thoughts at times. It's not like me to have my guard down enough to feel that way.

I keep thinking about what it means. Why would this man, who I don't know at all, make me this crazy? Why am I so attracted to him that it keeps me up all night? Not even my trusty bullet took the edge off. I still want to fuck his brains out.

"Are you all right?" my mother asks with her hand on my arm.

"Yeah, sorry. Just had a long night."

"Work, I hope."

She stopped asking if it was a man after the time I told her it was actually two men.

That was an epic conversation.

I nod. Callum is technically work. "I have a big project on the horizon. One that even Dad might be impressed with. He's supposed to have the contract drawn up based on our negotiations last night."

Her eyes have a hint of sadness layered in, and I don't have to ask why . . . I said *dad*. This is why love sucks. I may enjoy driving my mother batshit crazy, but seeing her still so hurt over a man who doesn't think twice about her—is sad. It's depressing that something we want to bring us some sort of wholeness ends up tearing us apart. That isn't what love is meant to do, yet that's what always seems to be the end result.

She recovers and smiles. "That's great about the project."

"Yeah, it is."

"Who is the company?"

"Dovetail," I say, knowing she'll know who that is.

"Wow, Nicole. That's impressive. I thought I read something about Martin Dovetail passing away."

"He did. I'm working with his son. Actually, you've met him."

"I have?"

I nod. "Yes. Callum was at the club the other night, do you remember?"

"The British gentleman?"

I would have gone with the hot-as-fuck British guy with a jawline I want to lick and eyes I want to fall into, but sure, British gentleman works.

My mother laughs softly. "Interesting."

"What is?" I say with a defensive tone.

"Oh, nothing. Just that you went all glassy-eyed and smiley."

I did not. "You need to see the eye doctor."

Her lips turn into a full smirk. "Okay. If you say so."

"We are not talking about this."

"About the fact that you like someone?"

Seriously? How did she jump to that conclusion? Never mind that she's right. I'll eat glass before I admit that.

"I don't like him."

"Okay."

"Seriously, Mom. I don't."

"If you say so . . ."

I groan. "Remember, I'm an only child and you're getting older. Who do you think is going to be shopping for your nursing home?"

She snorts. "Please, I'll escape daily to live with you. Come on, let's go grab lunch. We can argue about my living arrangements over a glass of wine."

Now we're talking. I link my arm in my mother's, and we walk out into the courtyard of the shopping center. There are a few great swanky restaurants that we frequent often in this area, but I steer her toward our favorite little pizza place.

Mom and I chat about an idea she has about doing some redesigning to her living room, which I helped her design a little over a year ago. I don't know if it's boredom or what, but it's really confusing how she continues to redo her home.

The waiter brings over the food, and she digs in while I look around. I love coming here. Not because it's a place only locals go but because as pretentious as my mother is sometimes, she'll eat pizza like a champ.

"It's been too long since we've been here," she says as she takes a bite.

"You know, I'll never get used to seeing you when we come here."

"Why?" she asks with her brow raised.

"Because you're so . . . proper all the damn time. But stick a slice of pizza in front of you, and suddenly, you're normal."

She puts her slice down and pats her lips. "No matter how many years it's been since I've lived in New York, that part of me will never disappear. Had things worked out different for me, you would've been raised there."

Ahh, the story of my father stealing her life. Here it comes. "I know, Mom."

"No, Nicole, you don't. New York is something that lives inside you. I know you think it's crazy, but that city breathes life. It's full of everything. You experience so much in one minute that it can take you a lifetime to ever truly accept it."

"I worry about you."

She shakes her head with her eyes closed. "One day, you'll find something that is too much and not enough all at once."

My heart slams against my chest. The past and present do a dance in my heart as I think about Andy and Callum. Andy made me feel everything at once. It was like being in that carnival ride where it spun so fast you were smooshed against the side. I never felt centered. Callum does a little of the same, but as of now, I don't feel like he's going to leave me dizzy. The fact that I had even a glimpse of that is why I ran. I always want to be on steady ground.

"It's . . ." I start, but something catches my eye.

A man in a dark suit enters the pizzeria. My body knows who it is before my head does.

"Nicole?" Callum's accent practically croons my name.

"Callum." I attempt to smile but probably fail. I can't feel my face. "I thought you were in London?"

"I'm clearly not." He smiles and then looks at my mother. "Mrs. Dupree."

"Hello, Callum. It's lovely to see you again." She stands to greet him.

"You too." He kisses her cheek.

"Please, have a seat." The traitor formerly known as Mom invites him to join us.

"He can't," I say quickly. "I'm sure Callum has somewhere else he needs to be."

"Actually, I don't. I'm staying in the States another few days. I extended my trip to handle some additional things."

Of course he did. "Oh. That's wonderful," I say through gritted teeth.

"Yes, I was going to call you today to discuss some ideas about the project."

"Oh?" Mom cuts in. "That's right. Nicole said you guys were working together."

That is not what I said. "We haven't signed anything yet," I correct her.

There's a little issue on whether or not I'm going to work *for* him—which I'm not. The contractor thing is appealing, but until that gets completely worked out, there's no job as far as I'm concerned.

"Yes," Callum agrees. "Not yet, but I have a feeling we'll come to an agreement."

Smug bastard.

"You hope."

He laughs. "Yes, I do hope. You're very talented, and it would be a shame not to be able to come to some sort of resolution, don't you think?"

I go to open my mouth with a smart-ass remark and then remember that's probably not the best idea. We don't have anything in writing, after all. "Yes, it really would."

Mother sniggers and then clears her throat. "You know, I just remembered that I have to meet my friend in an hour."

She is so full of shit.

"You said you wanted to spend the day together. You never once mentioned a friend."

She attempts a forlorn smile but sucks at it. This is why she didn't get very far in acting. "I know, but it slipped my mind. You know how it is when you get older . . ." My mother touches her chest as though she's so sad about it.

"Well, we can take the pizza to go," I offer.

"No, no. Don't do that on my account, sweetheart." Her hand touches mine.

"It's fine."

My mother turns to Callum. "Do you mind spending the day with her, Callum? We just got our food, and as you can see, Nicole hasn't eaten a thing."

Oh. My. God. She didn't. "Mother!"

"I don't mind at all." Callum grins at me.

"I'm so sorry, sweetie." She comes over and kisses my temple. "I'll make it up to you. I promise."

"Oh, you so will," I warn.

And just like that, my matchmaking mother has gotten her damn way. And so has Callum.

eleven

. . .

Nicole

"WELL, this is an interesting turn of events," Callum chuckles.

"Is it now?"

"What does that mean?"

Please, I'm not stupid. I know exactly what the hell is going on. He's clearly obsessed with me. "You just happened to come to *this* pizza place in Tampa? A place you know nothing about?"

"You think I'm following you?"

"Yes, I think you're following me," I say, mocking his accent.

"That's bloody rich." He laughs.

"Right. It's a little scary."

Callum looks at me with humor in his eyes. "It is because, clearly, you're following me."

"Umm, I was here first."

"Maybe today, but I assure you, not every other day that I've frequented this restaurant."

I purse my lips and stare at him. What the hell? He's not following me? "This is just a coincidence?"

He shrugs. "Call it what you want, but I don't need to chase you. You wear your attraction to me very openly."

Please, he thinks he knows me?

Yeah, I don't think so, buddy. I will never admit defeat.

"Attraction?"

"Yes. You want me. Let's not pretend. I don't know many women who rub a man's cock if she's not interested. Which you are."

"Not likely."

Maybe he has some sort of mind reading ability? Or maybe I suck at hiding that I undress him constantly? Either way, denial is not just a river in Egypt, it's here, too, and I'm floating down it.

"So, just now, you don't wish that you'd gone back to my place that night?"

"Nope."

Lie.

"You don't wish you knew exactly how it felt to have spent the night with me?"

I squeeze my legs together and level him with a stare. "No."

"If you say so . . ." Callum trails off.

"Please, I'm not the one following you around."

He shakes his head, leans in, and drops his voice. "I spent all my holidays from school in Florida since I was three years old. I know this place because my father owned the businesses on this street. I've been eating here since I was a just a tot."

Now I feel like a total asshole. "Well, okay then. That makes sense, I guess."

He smirks while sitting back in his chair. An older gentleman comes around the counter, with his arms open and eyes warm. Callum does the same and they both embrace while the other man claps Callum on the back. "It's been too long, son. Too long since you've come to see your Uncle Gio."

Callum nods and returns the man hug with the customary back slap. "I was here the other day, but you weren't, and you know why I couldn't come before that."

"Well, water under the bridge. You're here now."

"Yes, and I have company," Callum says with a smile.

"Who is this beautiful woman?" Gio's warm eyes turn to me.

"This is Nicole Dupree. She's the girl I'm planning to win over."

Great, the whole not sleeping together or dating thing didn't sink in.

Gio nods, and my lips part. "I see, well, Nicole, you're in for a ride with this guy. I've known him for a long time, and I've never seen him fail."

"I don't plan to this time either," Callum informs me.

Why does that statement make me want to both jump his bones and run? He's even sexier when he's broody and arrogant. Bastard. I have to stay strong. There are solid reasons why even this lunch is a bad idea. I don't know anything about Callum. He could be taken for all I know. Sure, he doesn't wear a ring and he hadn't mentioned anyone else back home, but I know as well as anyone that it doesn't really matter.

I lean back in my seat and cross my arms, ensuring my voice is as strong as my will. "Well, you're not the only player in this game. I think you'll find I'm a rather worthy opponent."

Gio laughs. "Maybe you've finally met your match. I like this one, Cal."

The nickname stops me. I just can't picture anyone calling him anything other than Callum. The name Callum is strong, power-ful, sexy as fuck.

"Cal?" I ask.

Callum rolls his eyes. "Only three people in the world can call me that, Gio, Milo, and my stepfather. Well, I guess my mum does, but it's very rare she calls me Cal, although I would never stop her."

I smile. "Well, *Cal*, we'll see if there's anyone else to hit your list."

He shakes his head and offers me a panty-dropping smile. "Not happening, love."

The term of endearment does something it shouldn't be allowed to do since I'm strictly not going there. I shouldn't like the way the letters rolled off his tongue. I shouldn't want to hear it again and again, maybe even record it so I can hear it whenever I want. None of that should be happening inside me, but it is.

I don't like this. I need it to stop.

"Well, I really need to get going," I say as I get up.

His hand shoots out, gripping my wrist, and electricity courses through me. I pull my hand back, needing to break the physical connection, but when my eyes cut to his, I see it written all over his face. He sees it too. His pupils are dilated, and his breathing is slightly accelerated. I cannot go there again.

"Please don't leave."

"This isn't a good idea," I say, holding on to the very little amount of self-preservation I have left.

"What? Eating a meal?"

I close my eyes and sigh. "We both know that's not what I'm talking about."

Callum gets to his feet, his height dwarfs mine, as does his presence. "I promise to behave. This is just lunch. What can be the worry in having a lunch together?"

It isn't just lunch, it's my traitorous heart and body that can't seem to stop wanting him. It's that, when he walked in, my stomach tightened and my heart raced. It's all the things that scare me because he's my damn client. He's also this mystery and someone I, Nicole Dupree, ran the hell away from. That is not normal. That is not okay, and I can't let myself fall for him.

I look up, loving the deep pools of blue that reflect back at me, and I hear the hint of confusion in my own voice. "It's not just you I worry about."

"What would make you feel more at ease?" His voice is calming, lulling me into a false security.

I can't let myself fall into this trap. "Nothing. I've done this dance, and I ended up with a broken ankle. I won't do that again."

He brings his hand up to my face, brushing my hair back. "I don't want anything, Nicole. All I want is for you to relax. I'm not going to hurt you. I won't push you." The sincerity rings true in each word. "I'm asking you to stay, have some pizza, and if you still want to leave when we're done, I'll understand. But Gio's pizza is best eaten in the company of another."

Ugh. Damn him. Now I feel like a crazy person because he really hasn't done anything wrong. He's been kind and polite, and I'm a loony person. I am *not* the loony person in my life. I'm the level-headed, sex-enjoying, fun friend. I do what I want with whomever I want and live a fucking joyous life. This guy has turned me into one of my crazy friends.

"Fine," I say with defiance. I'm going to eat pizza and then be like, so long, big guy. That's what a badass does. "I'll sit, but if you do anything flirty, I'm gone."

He raises his hands. "No flirting."

"Okay."

We both take our seats, and Gio comes back around the counter with bruschetta, fresh mozzarella, and slices of bread. "Thanks, Uncle Gio."

He smiles at Callum. "Did you know Callum is the reason Periano Pizza is open?"

"I didn't," I say as I take a bite of the bread that's been dipped in red sauce. "Oh my God!" I burst out. "This is heaven in my mouth."

Callum nearly chokes on his food.

"Mind out of the gutter," I tell him and turn back to Gio. "This is amazing. I've only ever had the pizza here, but this mozzarella with the sauce is unbelievable."

"Thank you, it was my Grandpa Vito's recipe."

"Well, it's fantastic," I say and then shovel a forkful of the mozzarella into my mouth.

He nudges Callum. "I like this one. A woman who can eat is attractive."

I smile. "Well, I should be damn near irresistible after this meal. I plan to lick the plate clean."

Callum's eyes meet mine. "I think that ship has sailed."

I point with my fork at him. "No flirting."

"I'm doing my best." His hands go up in surrender.

Whatever.

"I don't know if I would have the strength not to flirt," Gio smiles.

"Believe me," Callum says with strain, "it's rather difficult, but she's collaborating with me on a project, not dating, which she likes to make crystal clear."

I shrug. "No dating clients. It's a rule I live and die by."

Callum grins. "We'll see about that."

After an amazing lunch, where Gio spoiled me rotten, Callum asked if I would show him one of my favorite places. So, we're at the beach. My safe, calming, and soul-soothing place. Whenever I'm down or feeling off, I come here to find my center. It's where I can let go of my issues, pretending the tide takes them when it leaves.

"You really spent summers here every year?" I ask as we walk along the shoreline. He seemed almost surprised when we came here, as if he'd never seen the ocean.

"I did. My father insisted I spent time in America. I was mostly in Georgia, but we came to Florida for two weeks each summer to check on his businesses here. His sister lived in Tampa which is what made him buy up property. I didn't actually enjoy the area, though. I never got to see it."

"That seems so sad. That you didn't really get to do much."

It's crazy how much our childhoods mirror each other's. My father enjoyed toying with my mother, he was always selfish with his wants instead of mine, and he was miserable most of the time.

"I've never seen the ocean like this," Callum says as he looks out.

"Never? You never came to the beach?"

He looks off at the water. "I didn't get to see the ocean unless I was looking through a window. My time here was always about learning what my mother didn't care to teach us. Things like how to take a company and turn it to profit. You know, what every seven-year-old boy wanted to know when visiting his father . . ."

My heart breaks for the boy in him. "I understand that more than you know. My father is a brilliant businessman as well. I never did fun things when it was his time with me. He was either working or I was stuck with my temporary mommy while she used his black card to redecorate what the last one did. I think it's just how successful men who run empires are."

Callum turns to me with soft eyes. "Not all of them."

He's saying so much more than the words. He's saying he isn't that way. He wouldn't do that to his own child. I don't know how I know all of this about him, but it's there. I can see that Callum would be there in other ways that our fathers weren't.

"No, I guess not. Maybe it's a choice."

His hand reaches out, and for some reason, I take it. It's like two broken children just found something together. His thumb brushes against the top of my hand, and I become dizzy. Why does his touch always feel so right? Why am I so lost one second and then so found the next when he's around? It makes no sense. We barely know each other, and yet, I understand him.

"I will never treat a child that way. I had the complete opposite at home with my mum. My stepfather was the one who took Milo and I everywhere. He always made sure that the only thing we always had was fun."

I love that he had that. "My mom never remarried. My father broke her heart so badly that I don't think she could ever find all the pieces."

Like someone else standing on this beach.

"I'm sorry for her."

I shrug and pull my hand back. Not wanting to seem like it was because of that moment that I did it, I pull my hair up into a messy bun and start to walk again. "It's fine, she's happy taking his money and irritating him. What is your mom like?"

He smiles, and I think this will be nothing like my feelings toward mine. "She's wonderful. She is a great mum even though she had a lot of pain in her life. The complete opposite of my biological father. Warm, caring, always smiling as though she couldn't stop herself. She had to endure a man who wasn't capable of loving her or the son she loved more than her own life. I can't imagine that was easy for her, so even if she has flaws, which she does, she did the best she could."

I wish I could see things the way he does. I love my mother, I really do, but she drives me nuts. "Mine is a handful."

He laughs. "Yes, it seems your mum and you aren't close?"

"It's not that we're not close, it's that we're very different."

"How so?"

I sigh. "Besides her being crazy when it comes to how I live my life? She's very judgmental about me."

"What about?" Callum pushes.

I really hate talking about her. I usually end up angry, but Callum was just open, and in some small part inside me, I want to do the same with him.

"She wants me to be married and popping out kids. I want none of that. I'll never get married because monogamy is ridiculous. Who the hell wants to be with one person for the rest of their life? No one. We delude ourselves into thinking that this is what we're supposed to do, and you know what? Most don't."

Callum stops walking. "You're quite passionate about that, I see."

One day, I'll be able to control my tongue. Clearly, that day isn't today. "I just . . . I don't want to tie someone down who doesn't want to be. I've seen what happens firsthand when there's one person who wants out but isn't mature enough to actually leave."

That's the best I can come up with. I would rather have zero expectations about a relationship and be surprised than have lofty expectations and end up hurt. My friends all thought their marriages were going to work and that was not the case. It's better to be guarded than think love is sunshine and unicorn poop, because it's not, love sucks.

"That's fair, but what if you meet a man who wants to marry you, love you, and be devoted to you? There are men like that who exist."

Ahh, the question that has no answer since it's impossible to know the future. "Well, I'd ask him to flash forward in his time machine and show me how he feels in ten years, five, or even a month from that date. Chances are, he doesn't feel that way again."

He laughs. "So, you don't believe a man can love a woman his entire life?"

"Yes, no . . . I'm not sure. It's that unknown that keeps me from trying."

And that I was a mistress and will never be the wife who is oblivious.

"That's rather sad," Callum says softly.

"I think it's smart."

"Sure, but at what cost?"

I shrug. "I think I'm fine. I have a great job, a wonderful home, unbelievable friends who have even more unbelievable kids. I have a very healthy sex life, and I'm happy. If the cost is that I'm not going to get my heart trampled, then that's fine by me."

Callum grabs my wrist, stopping me from going forward. "What if that man would give you more than you knew you could have? What if his touch made you faint in the knees? His love made you stronger instead of weaker? What if he protected you, keeping you from any pain because his life's mission was just to make you smile?"

My heart races because I wonder if that is real. I close my eyes, letting the vision of Callum's arms protecting me filter in. I allow the little movie to play out in my mind of us ten years down the road, wrapped up in a blanket on the beach as our kids played in the sand. His love cocooning me in a way I never thought possible.

When I open my eyes, I remember that I was naïve before when I thought the same with Andy, and the movie screen goes black.

"That's a fantasy," I tell him. "One that usually ends with tragedy. It's better to just watch porn and call it a day."

He chuckles. "Even a good porn movie ends with a happy moment."

"Yeah," I agree with a grin. "They both orgasm, which is the best ending you can get. And the only one I'm ever going to let play out."

twelve

. . .

Callum

IT'S QUARTER AFTER ONE, and I can't sleep. All I can think about is Nicole. We enjoyed a few hours together on the beach, laughing, enjoying each other's company and then I knew I had to back off. I remembered her offhanded comment in the restaurant about her broken ankle. Then, as she talked more about her feelings on love, it became clear she'd been hurt.

Today was a huge coincidence that worked to my benefit. I had planned to go see Gio since I'd been in town long enough without visiting. It'd been a long time since I'd stopped by, mostly because I knew there would be disappointment at my lack of communication. He's the only man in America who ever felt like family. My father was more of a business partner, but Gio always offered me a friendship. Even though now, I guess he and I are business partners as well.

Ten years ago, my father decided he was going to sell the real estate he owned when his sister died. He didn't care about the people it would effect. No, he only cared about further lining his pockets by selling to a developer who was going to tear it all down. I knew that it meant Gio would lose the pizza place, and I couldn't allow it.

I bought it from dear old Dad under a shell company and gifted the use of the building to Gio. I was able to keep that quiet for about five years until Milo's big mouth ruined it.

I was there on the street, debating whether I should go in, when I saw her sitting inside, and I couldn't stop myself. I wanted to be where she was. It was a gamble whether she'd think I was crossing the line, but at the same time, I had to be close to her. Then, when her mother offered to leave, there was no doubt in my mind I would do whatever I could to spend some time with her.

I get out of bed, splash water on my face, and call my brother.

"What the fuck are you doing awake?" Milo answers the phone. "It's one in the morning there."

He's a genius. "I'm aware of the time, I can't sleep."

"Clearly."

"What's going on at the office?" I ask, wanting to get some work done since I'm awake anyway.

Milo runs over a few details on the projects we have going on. Thankfully, my staff there is capable of keeping things running without me there. This company doesn't have that infrastructure yet. Nothing was done by others, he had his hand in every facet of his business.

I take the opposite side of how to run things. I believe trusting others is part of what makes you a good boss. You have to give people the lifeboat and hope they paddle to shore.

"When will you be back?" Milo asks.

I should be there right now. I planned to be back, but I'd be lying if I said I didn't want to leave. Mostly because, for the first time in a long time, there's someone I want to be around.

"When I get things situated here," I tell him. Vague answers are the best when it comes to my brother. If he thought I was returning tomorrow, he'd be off in the Greek Isles by sundown.

"And how long will that be?"

"I don't know, Milo," I snap. "There's a lot of things I'm juggling. You're going to have to do what's necessary there or I'll find someone else who is willing to step up."

I start to pace, gripping the back of my neck. I knew this day would come at some point. Knew I was the only heir to my father's estate, but I wasn't nearly as prepared to take it over as I thought. What has me so on edge is my company in London. Dovetail is thriving there. It's my dependable income, and while the US company is doing better, it's a lot of gambles. I like a sure thing. It's Milo who usually talks me into the risks.

Milo clears his throat. "All right, Cal, no need to be a bloody prick about it. Fuck, just keep me informed."

"I will."

My brother switches gears. "So, meet any hot women since you've been there?"

Immediately a vision of Nicole flashes before me. She's driving me mad. I think about her smile, her voice, the way her aqua-colored eyes change based on what she's wearing, and how she brushes her hair back when she's slightly nervous.

"I've been rather busy with work." I can't tell him. He's like a dog with a bone.

"I forget, you're all work and no play."

"Unlike you, who thinks only with your cock and never your brain."

Milo chuckles. "Maybe, but at least my cock gets the fun."

"Idiot."

"Jealous?"

Yes, but I won't tell him that. My brother has had everything in life handed to him. My mother babied him whilst I had to work twice as hard for everything. He's ten times smarter than I am, but couldn't manage to get good grades because it meant he had to actually put the work in. I spent hours studying and still struggled. Milo has no idea how jealous I am of him most days.

"I'm going to try to sleep now," I tell him, wanting off this call.

"Sure you are. Give me a ring tomorrow, and I'll have the numbers for you."

I don't bother to tell him it is tomorrow for both of us because it won't change anything. I'll be happy if I get them by next week.

"Talk to you then," I say and disconnect.

I fire up my laptop and start going through emails. I'm keyed up and pissed off, and I don't even know why. Before bed, I cleaned out all important messages, within a matter of four hours, I have over a hundred new ones.

People wonder why I never take a vacation, this is why.

I delete a bit of junk, and then I see a name that causes my pulse to spike.

Nicole Dupree.

I open the email and smile.

Callum (Cal),

Thank you for the pizza today, it was amazing. I had a great time, and now that we've had some time together, I know you a little better and will be able to come up with some great designs.

I know you mentioned staying in the States a bit longer, so I wanted to see if we could have a meeting at my office on Friday? I should have some preliminary designs by then.

Best,
Nicole

First, she called me Cal, which I hate, but coming from her, I don't mind. Second, she enjoyed today, and that is a victory. Third, she wants to see me again. All of these are wins in my column.

I can't explain why these small things make me grin. In just one look, this woman got under my skin. She bewitched me, and I can't stop thinking about her.

The timestamp from the email says she sent it ten minutes ago. Apparently, I'm not the only one up late.

Now, I need to be strategic and get her to agree to another day like today. I want her to see me, know me, and get out of her head. I don't give a shit if I'm her client. I'm a man first, and I want her.

I know she wants me as well. Whatever stupid rules she has, I plan to make her forget.

Nicole (Nic),

You're welcome for the meal, it was my pleasure. It seems my uncle was enamored with you as well since I've never seen such service before. I, also, enjoyed our time together. I do plan to stay in the States longer— mostly because I can't seem to want to leave you.

A meeting would be great. However, why don't we do it over dinner? This week is busy with meetings, but I'm free later on in the evenings.

Sincerely,

Callum (not Cal)

I re-read the email, delete the bit about not wanting to leave her because it doesn't seem appropriate, and then send it.

Then I wait.

Sure enough, I get a response back.

Cal,

You seem to like dinner meetings a lot. That's fine. I can do Friday night. By the way, why are you awake?

Best,

Nicole (definitely not Nic)

I'm grinning ear to ear as I respond.

Nicole,

I prefer not to eat alone, and if I can do it in the company of a beautiful woman, even better. Why don't we do tomorrow instead? Friday is too far away, and I may be leaving before then.

I'm awake because I can't sleep. What about you?

Sincerely,

Callum (note that I didn't call you Nic . . . that should account for something.)

Another email in minutes.

Callum, (you're welcome)

I won't have designs done by tomorrow. It would be a frivolous meeting, and I'm sure you're too busy for those. You know, running the empire you have and all. Let's do Wednesday, that's the earliest possible time I can manage. Is that okay?

Also, I figured you couldn't sleep since you were emailing. I can't get something off my mind, and it's keeping me up.

Best,

Nicole

. . .

I know I promised her no flirting, but something niggles in my stomach, telling me that she needs to be pushed. I like to pride myself on knowing how to read people, but Nicole is a mystery.

The night we met, I swore I would've had her under me, screaming my name, clawing at my back. I would've worshipped her body, and we could've parted ways. I'd never met a creature like her before, and I was desperate to have her. Every sign pointed to a night neither of us would've forgotten.

But she ran.

She ran, and I'm determined to find out why.

Something scared her, and truth be told, I was terrified that I would not want to let her go once I had a taste.

She isn't the girl you walk away from. I knew that the moment I saw her.

Whatever spooked her is fine because I've never been afraid of the chase.

I grab my phone and dial her number.

thirteen

. . .

Nicole

WHAT THE?

Why is he calling me?

Shit.

He knows I'm awake. I can't *not* answer since I just sent him an email three minutes ago. Damn it. I have to be a grown-up and pretend like I didn't wake up in the middle of the night after having one hell of an erotic dream of him.

Okay, deep breath and answer the phone. You can do this. You are the fucking badass in your life, and this is just a stupid man with a big dick . . . you got this.

"Hi, Callum," I say as though I wasn't freaking the fuck out.

"Nicole. I figured this was easier."

I snort. "What's up?"

"We are."

I laugh at the stupid answer. "That's true. Did you need something?"

Other than a really good night of fucking . . .

"Coffee. I need coffee. My loft doesn't have enough and I was hoping you might know where I could go for some."

I put my laptop to the side of the bed and think. "Hmm, there's not much open right now, besides, maybe it's best to go back to sleep . . ."

"I doubt that will happen."

"I'm the same. Once I'm up . . . I'm up."

"It's a curse, really," Callum says, and I picture him in a pair of shorts, no shirt, with messy bed head.

God, he's fucking hot. I wish he were here. I would recreate that damn dream in 4k UHD and surround sound. We'd break things while tearing each other's clothes off. I'd bruise and not give a shit because it would be unbelievably off the charts. He'd burn me alive, and I'd take every lick of the flame.

"Why don't you come over here? I have coffee," I say and immediately clasp my hand over my mouth.

What the fuck was that? Oh my god. I freaking invited him here at one thirty in the morning. Jesus Christ.

He doesn't reply, probably as taken aback by what I said as I am. After another second of silence, I give him an out—well, me an out.

"You don't have to. I was just—"

"I'll be right over."

Great.

"Okay, for coffee," I clarify.

"Yes. For coffee."

And hopefully breakfast.

No. No breakfast. No nothing. Just coffee.

I don't say anything and he clears his throat. "Nicole?"

"Yes. Sorry."

"Text me your address."

"Okay," I say and then hang up the phone. In the back of my mind I know this is a bad idea, but too late to back down now.

Dear God, let me keep my pants on.

I take a very cold shower to try to cool down before he arrives. It's been fifteen minutes and ten almost text messages trying to bail out. All of them sounded lame, and I figured it was best to suck it up, keep my distance, and hope this will all be just fine.

Maybe.

My doorman was informed of Callum's visit, so now I wait.

Since my friends have no issue driving me nuts, I decide Kristin will be the recipient of tonight's text. Mostly because she would know why I'm having a mild panic attack.

Me: I know you're sleeping. But I have Callum on his way over here. My client, Callum. The guy I ran away from. I'm freaking the fuck out. You bitches never care about boundaries, so, here's me not caring. Call me. Now. Please. Call. Me.

My phone rings a few seconds later.

"Seriously?" she says half asleep.

"I'm crazy, right?"

"Was never even a question," Kristin says and grumbles. "What are you worried about?"

"Umm, sleeping with him. He's coming over for coffee," I inform her.

"Is that what the kids are calling it these days?"

She's stupid. "Not funny."

"No, what's not funny is you texting me that I need to call you because you have a booty call coming over."

It so is not that. She's missing the point. If it were a booty call, I'd have done a quick vag check on the shaving, did my hair, and perked up the boobs, but instead, I'm having a fucking meltdown.

"It's coffee, Kris. Coffee. No sex."

"Lies you tell yourself." She barely gets the jab out around a yawn.

"Why did I think you'd be the one to help the most?"

Kristin makes some noise in the background and then whispers to Noah. I hear a door close and smile. Good, she's up. "I don't know why you thought that, but my boyfriend is now going to make me pay for waking his ass up. That means you're going to pay. Look, you're freaking out because this is the first guy since the dickface to make you feel this way. The other guys you've done things with—things I try not to think about—were nameless faces. It was how you numbed your pain, and yes, you have pain."

Whatever. I have issues because men are dumbfucks who hurt women for play. "It's not like that."

"Stop lying to yourself. You spent the day on your most favorite beach with him."

"How—" I stop myself and then huff. "Fucking Heather."

"Yes, Heather told me, get over it. Point is, you like Callum, and you know what? That's good, Nic. It's really good. It means you have a heart that's not destroyed because of one person. Noah is the best thing that ever happened to me. He's the man I wish I could give the years I wasted with Scott. But you know what? I can't. All I can do is put that behind me and love him with all I am."

"What if Callum isn't the right guy?"

She sighs, and I picture her head tilted to the side as she answers. "Then you move on, but he could be everything. He could be the guy you've been waiting for. Don't close yourself off because of your silly rules. I swear it was you who said rules were meant to be broken."

I really hate it when my friends use my words against me.

"You've been super helpful."

Kristin laughs. "Good to know. Now, I'm going back to bed. You'll probably be doing the same soon enough?"

"I hate you."

"Feeling's mutual."

"Asshole," I grumble.

"Bitch."

It's funny because I am, in fact, a bitch. "I'll talk to you tomorrow."

"I can't wait to hear. I love you, Nicole. Don't let your past relationship determine the one in front of you. It's not his fault that Andy was a complete piece of shit. Go get laid and smile a little."

With that last tidbit, Kristin hangs up before I can reply.

Now, I need to decide what the hell to wear. Do I look cute and like I just woke up this way or do I want to look like I'm up and ready for the day?

Just woke up like this. Definitely.

I throw off my lounge pants and opt for really cute booty shorts with "sexy" written across the butt. I think it's fitting, and then I head to the bathroom. Not wanting to oversell myself. I toss my hair into a messy bun and throw some mascara on.

Once I'm pleased with my appearance, I sit on the couch and listen to Kristin's words bounce around like a pinball hitting the circles. There's so much to think about, but she's right. I'm basically dooming any man because *one* guy hurt me. Callum may not be the right guy for me, but what I do know is that it's never a good idea to shit where you eat.

So, until this project is done, no sex.

Maybe I should go change into something that hides my legs?

There's a loud knock on the door, and I jump.

Of course, I think about sex and then he shows up and I don't have an option to change either. I really have the worst luck with this guy.

I open the door with a smile, and I swear I almost fall over.

He's standing there in a pair of basketball shorts and a tight workout shirt that makes every single curve and dip in his chest visible. Jesus. Christ. I've died. As I make my way up to Callum's face, his lips turn to a grin.

"Good morning."

"Sure is," I reply. I don't even have the wherewithal to care that I'm totally flirting.

"Like the view?" he asks.

"I love things that rise, you know, the sun, heat, certain anatomy . . ."

Callum bursts out laughing. "I like you when you're unguarded at two in the morning."

I shake my head and pull the door open. "Come in. I have the coffee brewing."

He enters my apartment and looks around. "If I had any doubts about hiring you, they're gone now. Your place is breathtaking."

So are you.

"Thanks," I say instead.

He smiles. "Seems to me that all things pertaining to you are rather beautiful."

My cheeks heat, and I want to slap myself. I'm freaking blushing like a sixteen-year-old. Dear God.

"Flattery will get you everywhere, right?"

Callum chuckles. "That's what they say."

We head into the kitchen, and I grab two mugs. I'm all about convenience with everything—except coffee. I used to watch my mom with her coffee press and think: *Dear Lord, woman, get a coffee maker.*

Then I tasted it.

It's different, and once you have a little, you can't ever go back.

I pour us both a cup, and we sit at the eat-in area. "Here you go." I smile.

"Thank you. This already will be a million times better than the shit they have at the lobby of my loft."

"So," I say before I take a sip. "What had you unable to sleep?"

He shrugs. "A lot on my mind."

Oh, I know that feeling.

"Same here."

"You know, our list of things in common far outweighs our differences."

"Really?" I lean back with my coffee cup.

Callum takes a sip and then grins. "You're gorgeous, I'm rather good-looking. You have a father much like mine. You own your own company, as do I. You can't sleep, and neither can I. There's really only one thing we don't agree on."

I smile. "And what is that?"

"That we shouldn't explore whatever it is that's growing between us."

My heart starts to race, and I push my hair back. "Callum."

"Just listen." He puts his hand up. "I know you have rules. I have them as well." His voice is like warm sugar. "You're missing one important thing about all of this."

I lean forward, unable to keep the distance. He smells too good. His voice is too intoxicating. The way he looks is too much. I want him so badly that my insides physically hurt. He's the damn forbidden fruit, and I'm Eve, wanting to swallow that damn apple whole. I'm strong, but damn it, I feel weak.

"What am I missing?" My voice is husky, even to my own ears.

"I'm not your client yet."

And with that, he closes the distance and kisses me before I can do a damn thing.

fourteen

· · ·

Nicole

KISSING him is unlike anything else. I now understand the expression you have to kiss a lot of frogs to find your prince.

Callum's mouth is exactly what I like. Firm, yet yielding. Strong, yet gentle. And when our tongues touch, I swear I can't breathe.

My hands tangle in his hair, keeping him exactly where I want him. I don't care that while we technically haven't signed our contract, he's my client. I don't care that this is a bad idea. It feels too good.

Everything about this is right.

It's also so wrong.

He pushes the chair back before lifting me into his arms. We move until my back is pressed against the wall and his hard body is holding me captive there. Our lips don't break away while we both battle for power. Callum, however, doesn't relent. He toys with me, allowing me a moment to think I have control, but then it's gone before I can grasp it completely.

It turns me on even more.

"God, your mouth," Callum says, barely breaking away long enough to get the words out.

If there was ever a chance I could pick which way to die, it would be from this man's mouth. Take me to heaven because I'm dead.

His lips slide from my mouth, moving down my neck, and I close my eyes. "We should stop." I don't mean a single damn syllable of it.

"I disagree," he says as his mouth moves lower against my chest.

"This is a bad idea," I reiterate while pushing his head lower. Clearly, I'm just saying it to hear myself speak.

Callum's hands move from my hips up my sides, sliding his thumbs across my nipples. "I think it's the best idea we've had thus far."

He swipes back again, and I moan. "Maybe you're right."

His lips move up, grazing the spot right below my ear. "Oh, I know I am. Do you want me to stop?"

I shake my head.

"Do you want more?"

I look down at him, knowing there isn't a chance in hell I could stop this even if I wanted to, which I don't. "I want it all."

"Where's the bedroom?" he asks as he lifts me, causing my legs to wrap around his waist. The hard length of his cock presses against my stomach, and all I can think about is how good that *big* bad boy is going to feel in a few minutes.

"Down that way." I point to the hall, and he starts to walk.

My lips are against his neck, kissing my way up to his ear. "I've dreamed of this," I confess.

"Me too, love. I've thought of nothing else but having you."

For the first time in a very long time, I have butterflies in my belly. I'm so sure this man will wreck me, but I'm walking the plank anyway, pulling him along with me as we jump into the rough seas.

Because, let's be real, I'm going to end up going under, but hopefully, he can be my life vest.

Callum carries me to the bed, his solid frame hovers over me. "I didn't come here for this," he says. "I want you to know that."

He's full of shit. This is exactly what he came here for, and it's the only thing I've thought about.

"Then what did you come for?"

"I don't know. I just don't want you to think it is just about touching you, kissing you, fucking you until neither of us can move again."

Well, that is quite the image, and one I'm ready for.

My hands grip his biceps, and my voice drops to a sultry tone. "We both know you didn't come here for coffee, Callum."

His eyes go softer. "No, it wasn't coffee. It was you."

I touch his cheek, loving the stubble that pricks the pads of my fingers. "Just tell me one thing," I say as the last layer of my armor starts to fall. "Are you married?"

"No."

"Then no more talking, and once those papers are signed, no more touching. This is a one-time thing until I'm no longer working with you, understand?"

He doesn't say another word because his lips are far too busy against mine. I know this is probably a mistake, but Kristin is right, rules are meant to be broken. I'm a smart girl, and this is sex. I can handle sex. It's feeling things that scares me, so all I have to do is guard that part of myself, and I'll be fine. Right?

Right.

Sex with Callum is all this is. Yup. Nothing more. Just a week of built-up sexual tension that has now come to a full boil.

He leans back, tearing his shirt off as I do the same.

There's no finesse. Just need. Want. Desire that's pumping so fast I can feel the heat and sparks starting to build.

Callum cups my face and crushes his mouth to mine. His hands move down my back, unhooking my bra and tugging it free. I totally put it on before he came, trying not to look like I was hoping for this. His eyes drink me in as my breasts spill out.

"Fuck," he groans.

"You like?"

Callum cups them both, kneading, and my head falls back as I rest on my elbow. "I like everything about you. Your lips," he says and then kisses me. "Your breasts." He leans down and runs his tongue along my nipple. "Your heart." Callum's mouth moves to place a kiss right over the erratic thudding in my chest. "And I know I'm going to love your pussy."

I grin, knowing I damn well am going to like his cock. "Well, then why don't you put your mouth there and find out?"

The challenge causes his eyes to flare. Oh, yeah, this is going to be good.

He grips my thighs, pulling me forward so my head is on the bed. My shorts go flying across the room, and he tosses my legs over his shoulders. "Hold on, love, I'm about to see if I like the sound of my name as I fuck you with my mouth."

"Holy shit!" I say as his talented mouth goes where I've been dreaming of it being. His tongue presses against my clit, flicking in a rhythm that has my toes curling before he rolls it in his teeth. I don't know how long this goes on for, but I'm sweating. He drives me higher and then, right when I'm going to peak, he drops me back down.

I'm the mouse, and he's the cat, toying with me until he plans to go in for the kill. I fucking love every second of it.

"Callum, please, fuck!" I beg. *Beg.* For the first time in my life, I'm begging because I can't take it much more. I need to release.

Callum's only response is to slip a finger into the well of my body, pumping maddeningly slowly, and I know I'm gripping him tight. I need more. I need it all.

Then he pulls it out and rims my ass. When he breaks through the tight muscles, his teeth capture my clit again, and I'm done. I fall off the cliff, so far down that I can't see straight. I scream his name, curse words, and I'm not even sure what else because I'm pretty sure I blacked out.

When I finally come back to reality, he's above me with a shit-eating grin on his face. He lost his pants somewhere in the middle of that and put a condom on.

"How did you like hearing your name?" I pant, barely able to peel my eyes open enough to appreciate the man nestling his hips between my thighs.

"Jury is still out, I think I'd like to hear it when I'm inside you."

"I'm happy to oblige."

He leans down, lips against my ear. "And this will happen again, love. Mark my words. I'm going to fuck you so good that all your rules about us won't even matter. I hope you're ready."

I smile, grip his hair, and pull him back so we're eye to eye. "Bring it."

When he pushes into me, I realize I'm so done. I will never be able to quit him. It wouldn't matter if he was my client, my pastor, or my boss, I'm lost to him, and I may never come back.

———————

"Favorite color?" I ask.

"Green."

"Really?" I ask. Green is such a harsh color. I know I'm coming from a design aspect, but it's a clashing hue when you're doing anything.

He nods. "It's the color of money."

Such a guy answer.

"You?" he asks.

We've been lying in my bed, butt ass naked without even a sheet draped over us. We've covered all the basics and are now on to the fun questions.

"Gray."

"Okay, and you made a face at green?"

"It's a color I can do or make into anything. It's malleable, and I like that. For example." I roll over and grab the gray pillow we tossed off the bed. "This is gray, right?"

Callum nods, and I grab a plum-colored pillow.

"Now, when I put it next to this pillow, what do you see?"

"Gray and purple?"

"Yes, but the gray makes the purple become vibrant."

He leans in and kisses me softly. "I think you're vibrant."

"I think you're trying to go for another round," I counter.

"You would be correct."

As much as I want nothing more than another fantastic round of fucking, I need to come up for air. He's so damn good that I don't know if my body can handle another orgasm. The man has given me more than the last time I had two guys working for the same goal. That says it all right there. He's a God.

"Favorite food?" I say, pulling away so he doesn't get his hands on the goods.

He doesn't answer, he adjusts his half-cocked cock and clears his throat. "You tell me yours."

"That's a hard one. I'm a foodie, always have been, but I love Italian food the most."

Callum grins. "Me too, have you been to Italy?"

"No. I haven't traveled abroad as much as I'd like to. I was in the UK for a short trip with my dad on one of his promise-to-spend-more-time-with-me trips." I throw up air quotes around the last bit and roll my eyes. "He was so full of shit. He made it sound like he wanted to take me around Europe when all he wanted was to kill two birds with one stone. He ended up taking meetings almost the whole trip."

"Italy is one of my favorite places. The food, wine, and people make it unforgettable."

I lie on my back and sigh. "I envy you."

"Why is that?"

With my head turned, I smile. "Because you can just go to Italy so easily. All we have here is the beach and Caribbean. Don't get me wrong, I love them both, but they aren't exactly full of art and history. It's great because I can drive down to the Keys and find inspiration, but I love the whole design elements of Tuscany and Rome. It's rich and different from the beach feel I typically work on here. One day, I'll go. One day, I'll get to taste, touch, and experience it all."

Callum leans up on his elbow. "I guess you'll have to come with me to London."

"What?"

"You'll come to London with me next week, and I'll take you wherever you want to go."

I tilt my head at him. "I have to work on building your designs."

"You can work there."

"You're nuts!" I toss the pillow at him.

"Why?" he asks with a laugh. "You've never been, I love it there. There are a million places that could inspire you with all our rich history and designs. What possible reason could you have to refuse my offer?"

I try to find *all* the things I had in my bank of excuses, but I come up empty. "I don't know, but I'm sure there's a good reason, I just need to figure it out."

The truth is, I don't have anything. My friends don't need me. They're all married, dating, or whatever. My mother would love nothing more than for me to go on a European vacation with a millionaire. I swear she'd probably buy my plane ticket if it meant me going. I've already had to clear my entire schedule because I took this project on. There isn't a real excuse as to why I couldn't go.

Other than . . . he will be my client as soon as he signs the contract.

"Then I guess you'll be coming with me," he says as though it's decided.

I grin because I'm a dirty minded girl. "Oh, I think we'll both be coming together."

Callum catches on to exactly what I'm implying and moves toward me. "Do you now?"

"For sure."

"I bet we could come a few more times."

"I think you're a very capable man and can make a good go at it, Mr. Huxley."

Callum prowls forward on his hands and knees and flips me onto my stomach.

"I guess you're about to find out, Ms. Dupree."

fifteen

. . .

Callum

"I UNDERSTAND THAT, Edward, but I'm not in London," I grumble as my cousin explains that, yet again, my brother has disappeared. "I'm not sure what you expect me to do about it."

If I was there, I would fucking kill him.

I don't care that he's living the way he wants, he has obligations to the company and a goddamn job to do. I've let him slide long enough.

"I'm telling you, Callum. This is a problem. I don't mind stepping up and covering for the idiot, but at the same time, you should be aware."

"He's not going to like the outcome, that's for sure."

For someone who is bloody brilliant, he can sure be a stupid arse. I've reached the end of my patience with him, and there are a lot of things I've been pondering regarding being a CEO to two major corporations. It should be fairly easy considering I've spent the last decade trying to groom my brother. Instead of him stepping up, I have an entirely new set of issues because Milo is fucking reckless.

How do I split my time between two companies on two

different continents? Do I sell off my father's company and return to London? Do I leave London, which is full of awful memories, and get a start fresh? Start something with the blonde I can't get out of my brain?

Am I a bloody fool for even trying to pursue a woman I hardly know? Yes, I am, but I don't give a fuck.

Edward clears his throat. "If you need me, I'm here to step in."

He's been doing a lot of that lately, picking up the slack Milo leaves in his wake. "I know this, Edward. Believe me, I do. There's going to be some changes, and I'm going to ask you to step up a bit more."

As much as it pains me to do it, I think this is the only thing that will make Milo see I'm done with his games. I need someone I can rely on—all the time. Not only when it suits him.

"I'm happy to do it, Callum."

"I'll be in touch," I say and toss the phone on my desk.

I pace around my father's—*my* office and grip the back of my neck. I don't know how my life flipped completely. Edward is a second cousin and not even close to the type of person I'd like to leave in charge. However, he's the only one working, which is more than I can say about my brother.

Fucking Milo.

I grab the phone and send him a quick text.

Me: Get your bloody head out of your fucking arse and get back to work! I'm trying not to fire you, but so help me God, you're making it impossible.

Milo: I'm working whilst enjoying the sun.

Me: Do you want your numpty of a cousin to take your job?

It pains me to even type the words, but I need to know things are working while I'm here.

Milo: Don't make idle threats, Cal. It doesn't suit you.

Bastard.

Me: It's not a threat. Get back to the office or you'll find your job isn't what you once had.

A text message comes through, and my blood pressure is through the roof. People don't see the stress that comes with running a business. They only want to see the cars, houses, or whatever else comes with success. They don't see the sixteen-hour-long work-days, that I haven't been on holiday in four years, and that I don't have a single meaningful relationship.

All of that doesn't exist because my life is my business.

My world is making sure the people who work for me can pay their bills.

Whether or not Michael the mail clerk can afford his rent is dependent on Dovetail keeping its doors open.

That is the responsibility that rests on my shoulders.

Nicole: I've been thinking . . .

My chest tightens, but in a different way than it was before.

Me: I'm hoping this is a good thing. I've had a rather shit day.

Nicole: Well, I think it's good.

Me: Then please share.

**Nicole: My best friend is having a dinner party tonight and . . .
I need a date. Would you be interested?**

After everything that Nicole and I discussed, this is probably
something that is terrifying for her. She told me a lot the other
night about the four of them. How they are practically sisters and
how she values them more than anything.

I've never had friends like that, but based on what she said, I'm
quite jealous.

Also, it means she wants more time, just like I do.

Me: I'd love to.

Nicole: Okay, great. Meet at my place by six?

Me: I'll see you then.

I try not to smile, but I can't stop it. She reached out and isn't giving me her bullshit about rules and clients.

Maybe my stay will be extended even longer because I'm not returning to London if I have a chance with Nicole. No fucking way will I walk away from her that easily.

sixteen

. . .

Nicole

IT'S JUST dinner at Danielle's house. Not a big deal.

Danni offered to host this month's get together because Kristin's house is under construction and Heather is never around anymore. I sure as fuck wasn't doing it because I'm lazy and never do.

Of course, once I informed my asshole friends I was bringing a date—for the first time ever—they acted as if the Pope was coming. They started a group text, which I left *twice* and somehow got sucked back into, and proceeded to talk about how unicorns must be falling from the sky.

I really hate the whole payback excuse they continued to use.

My doorman rings up that Callum has arrived. I head to the door, opening it so I can wait for him.

The fact that I've seen him naked does nothing to quell the excitement of seeing him now.

"Hello, gorgeous," he says as he walks toward me.

"Hello, yourself, handsome."

Callum doesn't hesitate. He wraps his arms around my waist,

pulling me tight to his front, and his other arm slides up, wrapping around the back of my neck as he brings his lips to mine.

It's one of those kisses in a movie. Where the girl goes limp in his arms, but he holds her tightly, ensuring she won't fall. It's filled with magic and that big sigh because, with him, she's safe.

Just like I am.

Fucking hell, this is so not in the plan.

His mouth molds to mine, and there goes my damn dreamy sigh.

Far too soon, he pulls back.

"If I stay like that, we'll be rather late because you'll be under me while I'm deep inside you."

"Well, then, let's be late," I say with a grin.

He chuckles. "I would love to, but I'd like your friends to approve of me. I think it'll help when the contract is final and signed."

I shake my head. "It won't."

"Ah, I have faith."

"I'm telling you, Cal, it won't. I have rules, and since you've found some loophole and I happen to think you're a very sexy man with a giant dick"—I rest my hand on his chest—"I'm letting it happen. Once the contract is signed, there's no loophole."

Callum leans in for another kiss. "We'll see."

Stupid stubborn British sex stud. We'll see is damn right.

"Underestimating me is a very bad thing."

His lips turn up into the most dazzling smile. "Whatever you say, Nic."

I slap his chest playfully. "Ass."

"Are you ready to go or do you need to use the loo?"

"Loo?"

"Sorry, toilet," he says the word with difficulty.

I freaking love his accent and strange words.

"No, I'm good. Do you need to use the little boy's room?" I ask while batting my eyelashes.

"If I step foot in your apartment, love, we won't be coming back out. Especially if I remove my trousers."

"Promises. Promises." I grip his hand. "Let's go before I take you up on the no-pants offer."

We get into the car, and my nerves start to go crazy again. I'm starting to think someone has messed with my damn mind. My friends, men, and sex don't make me nervous, yet when I'm around Callum, I'm nothing but a ball of chaotic nerves and hormone-driven lust.

On the ride there, I'm quiet and focus on not running us off the side of the road. I think about how my friends will react to him. What if they don't like him? Do I really care? Why do I care at all when, in a few days, he'll *just* be my damn client?

Oh, because I'm lying to myself. That's why.

I pull up and Callum looks at me. "Are you all right?"

"I'm fine."

"You act as though you're about to feed me to the wolves." He laughs.

I shift in my seat. "No, they're actually all really great, it's me who is the wolf."

He laughs loudly and shakes his head. "Well, love." He moves in so our lips are barely touching. "I'll be happy to eat you tonight."

Jesus, I love dirty talk. I go to bring my lips to his, but he jerks back and opens the door.

"Bastard," I mutter, and the sound of his chuckle comes through the car, letting me know he heard me.

Here goes nothing.

He takes my hand, but when I try to pull away, his grip tightens. Okay, then, we're going in as a couple. That won't backfire on me.

Danielle opens the door before we make it up the stairs.

"Damn." She sighs. "I was hoping to catch you making out in the car so I had something to give you shit about."

I roll my eyes. "Sorry to disappoint you. Callum plans to go down on me tonight, maybe we can video it for you?"

He chokes, and Danni laughs. "I'll be sure to let Peter know you offered."

Callum's eyes meet mine with a mix of horror and awe.

I shrug. "We have no boundaries. Be prepared."

"It's nice to meet you, Callum," Danielle says with her hand extended.

"Wonderful to meet you as well."

We enter, and my jackass friends come rushing forward. "Hey, I'm Heather."

"Hello."

"I'm Kristin." She smiles warmly and then winks at me. Glad to see he passed her hot guy gauge. "This is Noah . . ."

"Frasier," Callum finishes, extending a hand to Kristin's boyfriend. "Big fan."

Oh, God. I forget that Noah and Eli are big deals in the real world. To me, they're idiots who make my friends idiots. Noah isn't some big movie star, he's . . . Noah. Eli, well, I spent much of my childhood dreaming of that man, but now, he's just my best friend's husband. After the first fart, he lost his sex appeal.

"Nice to meet you. God knows you must be a pretty good guy to deal with Nicole," Noah says before bumping my elbow.

"Watch it, pretty boy. I'll break your face," I warn.

"You could try."

"Whatever." I snort. "This is Eli Walsh. Yes, my friends seem to have a thing with famous people."

Callum does the customary greeting and then looks over at me. "You failed to mention all this in our talk about your friends."

"It's much more fun this way, don't you think?"

He kisses my temple, and I melt into his side.

Then I see my friends.

Shit.

"I'm going to steal Nicole," Kristin says, grabbing my arm. "We need to make the sangria, and she's the best."

Liar. Danielle makes the best sangria. This is her thinly veiled excuse to drag me away from Callum so she can ask me a million questions she's too polite to ask in front of him.

He nods, and the guys all walk over to Peter's humidor, where I'm sure there is going to be a lot of boring talk about cigars.

When we get through to the kitchen, the three of them turn on me.

"Holy crap!" Kristin says first. "You didn't mention how hot he was."

"Umm, I totally did. I also mentioned he's ridiculously well hung."

I don't know why this is something my friends shy away from. If he has a big dick, why aren't we talking about it? It's a good thing.

"Keep your voice down," Danielle chides. "Ava is in that boy-crazy phase, and Peter overheard her talking to her friend about the size of something. I'm pretty sure it was a boy . . ."

"Ohhh," I say, clasping my hands together. "I'll totally talk to her about size, circumference, *and* I'll make sure she knows that when she touches—"

Heather slaps me. "Dear God! You don't need to be her dick coach. She needs you to tell her how stupid boys are."

I scoff. "I'm clearly the bad aunt."

"Yes," Danielle agrees. "We know this."

"Wouldn't you rather she gets all her sex information from the right person?" I ask. If I had a daughter, I'd hope she had someone reliable instead of another fumbling teenager.

"I would rather she stay a virgin until she's thirty," Danni counters.

"Yeah, like you did?"

"Not the point."

I laugh and roll my eyes. "Yes, Callum is great. I'm sorry I didn't give you enough details."

"You must really like him," Heather says with wistful eyes.

Ever since she got married, she's been in this perpetually dreamy state. It's so weird. Eli must be really packing it and using it the right way.

"This is probably the only time you'll see him. So, get all your mushy, weird moments out of the way now. He found some workaround to us fucking a few times, but once I sign that paperwork, it's done. I'm not going to screw my client."

Kristin rolls her eyes. "Why not? I screwed my assignment. If I remember correctly, you were the one to encourage me to do so . . ."

Again with the words being tossed back in my face. Damn, they're good at this. "Not the same. You weren't getting paid by Noah. I'll be like a high-paid hooker."

"If the shoe fits . . ." Heather says with a smirk.

"Whatever."

"You clearly like the guy," Danielle says. "Plus, the accent is sexy as fuck."

"No shit! Why do you think I dropped my panties to begin with?"

My friends are not going to help me find excuses to get out of this situation. They're going to drag me down into all the lame explanations and try to convince me that I'm the crazy person for walking away. I can already see the writing on the wall. They could be right. My telling Callum we need to cool it when I'm clearly hot for him might be dumb, but it's also my life.

Kristin grabs a glass of wine and hands it to me. "I'm just saying that you like the guy. You don't usually give enough of a shit about whatever man you have sex with to bring him to our monthly dinner. In fact, you've never done it. So, take that for what it's worth."

I roll my eyes. "I think you need to stop talking to your advice columnist and dishing out advice. I love you three, I really do, but I'm a smart girl. I have a business to run, and I don't have a man to catch me if I fall."

The looks on their faces tell me they get what I'm saying. Heather and Kristin wouldn't have to blink if they needed money. Not that either of them take from Eli or Noah, but they wouldn't have to ask. Danielle doesn't work, but she's raising Ava and Parker. Their lives are solid because Peter busts his ass as a lawyer.

I don't have an Eli, Noah, or Peter. I have myself.

"We'll catch you," Danielle says.

Heather smiles. "We'll always catch each other."

"Always," Kristin thirds what they said.

We all link hands. "And forever."

———————————

"Are you sure you have to go?" Danielle asks, slurring her words a bit.

I laugh. "We could stay forever!"

Peter wraps his arm around his very drunk wife. "No, honey. You both need to go to bed."

"But I don't want to!" She pouts.

"Yeah, me either. Well"—I turn to Callum—"unless you're going to bed with me. If that's the case, I'm ready to go right now."

Peter laughs. "Good night, guys. Callum, if you're around this week, give me a call. I'd love to have a cigar and maybe some whiskey."

Callum smiles. "I'd like that. I'll give you a ring."

Aww how cute. Callum made a friend.

He hung out with the three guys all night. Except for the few minutes he was in the hallway with me. He pushed me against the wall, kissing me until I was damn near grinding myself against his erection, and then he walked off as if nothing had happened.

"Drive safe!" Danielle calls.

I turn to Callum. "Ever had road head?"

He laughs. "I'm afraid not."

"Oh." I giggle. "We're going to have fun."

"Every day with you is a bit of fun, isn't it?"

Too bad that fun is going to end.

No, I'm not going to think about any of that. I'm going to blow this man's mind while we drive. That is all I'm thinking about.

What's the saying? Don't look a cockhorse in the mouth? Or gift horse? Or cock in the hand? Whatever. Doesn't matter.

"Come on, gorgeous, let's get you in the car."

We start to walk toward the sidewalk and Callum's hand rests on my hip. I lean in, breathing in his sandalwood and bourbon cologne. "You smell good."

He chuckles. "You do too, love."

"Why do you call me that?" I ask.

Callum lowers me into the passenger seat and squats down. "Because you're lovely. You exude love, and I wonder if it's possible to keep my feelings for you from growing."

Now, I'm just drunk enough that I'm not one hundred percent sure that this conversation is happening.

"So, you think you could love me?" I ask.

"I think it's impossible not to."

I narrow my eyes. "You don't even know me."

"I know enough."

I laugh. "You have no clue how crazy I am. Trust me, I'm a girl not even a father could love."

Callum's big hand comes up and tenderly cups my cheek. "Then he's a fool."

My eyes close, and I lean my head into his touch. He's so strong that I wonder if he can carry the burden of being with me. I'm crazy, reckless, and mistrustful.

"Or maybe you are."

He presses his lips to mine. "I guess we'll find out."

seventeen

· · ·

Nicole

I ROLL OVER, and when my face hits something hard and warm, I pry my eye open, praying it's Callum and not some other guy.

I remember nothing after getting into the car. I think we talked, but I'm not sure. There was a lot of giggling, but then I think I closed my eyes and that was it.

He's looking down at me with a smile. "Good morning."

Ugh. Morning. "I drank a lot more than I thought," I croak.

"Yes, but you were adorable."

Great. "I take it we didn't have road head?"

He laughs. "No, comatose sex isn't really my thing."

"Good to know."

I look around the room and realize we are not at my apartment. Instead of soft ivory with hints of pink, this room is black with stainless steel everywhere. The floors are concrete and the furniture is extremely masculine. It's clear a woman has not touched this place.

I sit up, noting that I'm in my bra and underwear. "Gimme a quick second?"

He nods.

I rush toward the bathroom, hating that I didn't have time to brush my teeth and make myself look great before he woke up. My friends all think I'm nuts for never letting a man see me before I've primped a little, but I don't care. It's how I keep my allure. Since that's gone, I'm up for some damage control—and snooping.

Once I'm done doing my business, I look for any signs that he's a serial killer.

First, the medicine cabinet.

Advil.

Razors.

Cologne.

Deodorant.

All normal and necessary.

Being as quiet as I can, I close that and open the cabinet below, hoping there's a damn toothbrush somewhere and no chloroform.

"You okay in there?" Callum's deep voice scares the shit out of me.

My hand flies over my heart. "I'm good, just . . . do you have an extra toothbrush?"

"I don't. I wasn't planning to be here this long, but you can use mine," he offers.

"Gross!"

I hear his deep, throaty chuckle through the door. "Why? I've had my tongue in your mouth as well as other . . . places."

True, but toothbrushes are a whole other level of closeness. "Still . . ."

"I didn't expect overnight guests, Nicole. You can use mine if you'd prefer or not."

Well, damn it. I want to kiss him, but my breath tastes heinous, so I can only imagine how bad it smells.

I stare at his toothbrush and decide I can't. We aren't even close to being there yet. God gave me ten fingers, and I believe one was shaped like a toothbrush for this exact moment.

Quickly, I use my finger and scrub my mouth as clean as I can, swish some of the mouthwash I find sitting on the counter, and then head out.

He's sitting back on the bed in only a pair of lounge pants. Damn, he looks good.

"So, we came to your place?"

"I wasn't going to leave you at your loft while you were pissed. I thought this was safer."

"I was mad?" I ask as I climb onto the bed. Shit. I don't remember that at all.

Callum shakes his head. "Drunk. Pissed means drunk."

"Ahh, I didn't know that. I need a British dictionary." And then I smirk. I could use something else that's British and starts with dick. "You know?" I ask with mischief in my tone. "I'm a big fan of morning sex."

His eyes shift, and he raises a brow. "Are you?"

"Oh, yes. It's really how we should all start our day, don't you agree?" I move forward, not really giving him the option. I owe him, and really, my reasons are not completely altruistic.

Callum sits up a little straighter, and I climb on top of him. "I think waking up just like this was perfect."

"I bet I can make it better," I promise.

"I don't doubt that, love."

Why do I like it so much when he calls me that? Why does the way he says it make me feel cherished even though that's crazy? I really need to stop the nervous fluttering in my stomach so I can walk away from him until our business arrangement is done.

I have a great way to shut him up. I fuse my lips to his, and he groans. Our tongues duel, and this time, I'm going to stay on top. I need the control because I feel completely out of control in my head.

Using my weight, I shove him against the headboard, and straddle him. His cock is hard and hitting me in the best place. His fingers dig into my ass, and I kiss him harder while reaching behind myself so I can unclip my bra.

One thing that is not missing between us is passion. We have that in spades.

I move back, letting the scrap of material fall between us and his eyes turn to liquid pools of heat. "Nicole." He moans and then his lips are back on mine.

I reach between us and rub him through his pants.

However, that isn't what I want.

I slide lower, keeping my mouth in contact with his skin, kissing my way down to the promised land.

My fingers hook under the waistband of his pants, and I pull them down before doing the same to my panties. "I may have missed out on road head, but now you can focus without worrying about crashing," I say with a smirk.

"You're a fucking gift from God."

Damn right I am. "Let's see if you call out his name when I blow your mind."

I run my tongue around the rim of his cock, loving the sound that escapes from his throat. Instead of toying with him, I open my mouth and take him as deep as I can.

"Fucking hell!" Callum calls out.

I don't like to brag, but I'm really good at giving head.

I bob up and down, drowning in each moan and grunt that Callum makes. I suck him deep, hard, and use my tongue along the way. His hands thread in my hair, and I let him set the pace he likes.

"That's it, love. Yes." He grunts, completely lost. "Fuck. Your mouth feels so good. Take it deep," Callum commands.

I do exactly as he wants. I take him to the back of my throat, and water fills my eyes, but I don't stop.

"I can't hold back," he says.

The warning is appreciated, but my goal isn't to pop off. I push his hand off my head, and start to move faster.

"God, Nicole!" He yells out before losing it.

Once he's finished, he pulls me up. "Hi," I say coyly. "I got you to say something to God."

He doesn't grin or play coy. Callum looks ravenous, and I have a feeling I'm about to get eaten.

Sure enough, he crashes his mouth to mine, pushing me down onto the bed. His hands cup my breasts and he squeezes them, pinching my nipples. Then he pushes my legs up, hooking them over his arms. His cock slides against me, seeking entrance, and all I want is him inside me.

I don't want or need anything other than him to fill me.

"I need you," I pant.

"You're damn right you do," he says while brushing against my clit again with his cock. "But do you want me?"

I moan. "Yes."

"I need to get the condom," he says.

"No. Now."

I can't believe I'm saying it, but I want him too much to care. "I'm clean, on the pill. You?"

"Clean."

"Okay. Now. Get the fuck inside me. I need you."

"Enough to stop with your warnings of walking away?"

Is he seriously negotiating right now? "Callum, give me your dick."

He chuckles and then kisses me, still not doing what I said. "Tell me you're not going to walk away."

"Your. Dick. Inside me. Now."

"Say it."

His hand slips between us, and he starts to rub circles. "Look how much you want me." He smirks.

"Yeah, don't make me wait."

"Tell me you won't walk away."

Jesus Christ. This is torture. "I can't," I say breathlessly. I'm on fire. I need him to ease the pain from being burned.

"Then I won't sign the contract."

"Oh my God!" I moan when he takes my clit between his thumb and index finger. "You're killing me!"

"No, love, I'm securing what I want."

"And what's that?"

His eyes lock on mine. "You."

Damn it. I want to fight him, but I'm not strong enough. I care about him, crave him, want to be around him all the time. I think about what he's wearing, if he's lonely, and I wake up each night wishing he was with me. No matter how fast and ridiculous it sounds—it's true. I'm a stupid girl, but I'm falling for him.

If I haven't already fallen.

While I wrestle with this in my mind, his gaze stays locked on my eyes.

His hand moves back up to my face, pushing the hair back in a tender motion. "Say yes, Nicole. Say you'll be mine."

I open my mouth to refuse, but I won't lie to him or myself. "I vowed I'd never do this," I say with my heart on my sleeve. "It wasn't until I met you that I wanted to break it. Don't shatter my heart, Callum."

With that, he enters me, kissing my lips. "I won't. I promise."

I really hope not because, if he does, I won't ever come back from it.

eighteen

. . .

Nicole

I PRINT the tickets off for our first official date. He asked me to pick something I wanted to do during the day, and then he would take care of dinner. Callum didn't really ever get to enjoy anything around here, so I picked the most American thing I could think of . . . a baseball game.

Thanks to one of the guys who still has the hots for me, I was able to get us seats behind home plate against the Yankees.

Right as the printer spits out the last piece of paper, Callum knocks on the door.

"You look adorable," he says when he gets a glimpse of me.

Yes, yes I do. I did everything to make sure I was cute. I'm wearing a pair of jean shorts, a white top, with my favorite pinstripe jersey over it, and a ballcap. I look freaking sexy.

I stand here, allowing him to peruse the goodies—meaning me, and then take him in.

He's dressed in cargo shorts, a gray T-shirt that clings to every muscle on his delectable chest, and a baseball hat—though, his is for the wrong team. "You looked perfect other than that," I say, pointing to his hat.

"Aren't they the home team?"

"Yes, but they're not the Yankees."

"I wasn't aware we had predetermined teams."

"We do."

Callum laughs. "Well, I like this cap, and I'm sort of from Florida, so I pick the home team."

"I want to like you, but I feel like we're walking into a fight here. I'm really passionate about baseball, but when it comes to the Yankees . . . I'm downright scary."

"You'll have to deal, love."

I'm already regretting this. "I wasn't exaggerating when I said I'm scary. I was ejected from the last game, and I am hoping they don't have my photo up on a board somewhere so I can get in. Some asshole started taunting my beloved number two, and I told him to knock it off. He laughed, told me to sit my sweet little ass down, and proceeded to shout at my man. So, I did what any self-respecting Yanks fan would do . . . I threw my beer at him and then kicked his ass."

Callum's eyes widen. "I'm sorry, you what?"

"I threw my drink at him, leaped over the chair, and slapped his hat down over his eyes, and then I took his beer and dumped it on him for good measure. I got hauled out of the stadium. Big baby was crying about getting his ass kicked by a girl."

But that's what happens when you cross me. The Yankees are the only thing my dad gave a shit about, and he took me to every game when they were in the state of Florida. We never missed one. I was at the great players' final games in New York. I'm a diehard. I don't play.

"I'm not sure whether I should be scared or impressed."

"I get that often, but I'm not kidding, Cal. I won't hesitate to dump beer on you if you cheer gleefully if my Bronx boys don't come out swinging."

He laughs, pulls me into his arms, and kisses my nose. "Just when I think I can't find you any more endearing."

My nerves spike a bit since I know exactly how bad I tend to get. There is absolutely nothing endearing about me when I'm watching my team. "Seriously, I think you should forego the hat with the team's logo that is not mine."

"You can't be serious."

"Oh, but I am."

"I'm not taking it off," Callum says with a grin.

"Wanna bet?"

"Sure."

Shit. That wasn't what I meant. "No, I mean that I bet you will."

He nods. "I know what you mean, and I'm not taking it off. We'll make a wager. If your team wins, then you have to go on another date with me."

Again with the coercion. "Seriously, what is it with you and trying to secure your dates?"

"I like to know we have plans. Plans keep me relevant."

I shake my head. He's more relevant than I ever planned on him being, but I don't tell him that. "The only thing that will keep you in my good graces is if you become a Yankees fan."

His arms drop. "Well, then, I guess I'll have to find another way to win you over."

I glare at him. "We'll see."

"You have to eat a hot dog!" I tell him as we stand in line at the concession stand.

"I will not."

"What can you possibly have against hot dogs?"

The game has been amazing. Callum watched everything with

wonder. I can't believe that, with all the time he spent here, his father never took him to a game or anything. This was the best part of my childhood.

"They're disgusting."

"They're delicious!"

He orders a burger, and I get two hot dogs because I freaking love eating authentic stadium food. "It's all about the experience, Cal." I nudge him.

"Fine," he tells the girl at the counter, "I'll take a bloody hot dog as well since she's demanding it be done."

The girl smiles at me and then lingers on him a bit too long. I watch her with pursed lips, waiting for her gaze to meet mine so I can tell her in girl talk to back the fuck off. She finally looks over and at least has the decency to look contrite.

I know he's hot—even if he is really fucking dressed down—but have some manners.

"What was that look for?" Callum asks.

Great. He caught me. Oh, well. "I was telling her to stop looking at you."

"Why is that?"

"Because we're on a date," I say unapologetically.

"We are."

"Do you want guys staring at me?" I ask.

He shakes his head. "I don't care because I know that I can do this." Callum leans in, his hand grips the side of my face, his fingers tangling in my hair, and he crushes his lips to mine. It's a powerful, sexy, and toe-curling kiss that I don't want to stop.

His eyes are full of passion as he looks down at me. "I do like it when you do that."

"They can look, but I'm the only one who can touch."

I smirk up at him. "For now."

"Is that so?"

"I'm still on the fence about you," I inform him.

The truth is, I've hurdled over the fence and am running the bases with him. Other than his shitty taste in baseball teams, he's sort of amazing.

"And what is keeping you on the fence?"

I shrug. "There are a few things I'm still waiting to decide."

Callum leans in so his lips brush my ear. "Perhaps tonight, after I've fed you, I'll change your mind . . ."

I step back, looking up into his eyes. "Perhaps you will."

He raises his brows, and I don't need him to say a word to hear what he's saying.

I'm going to cut the fucking fence down.

I can't wait to see what that looks like.

Don't play games that you can't win, Nicole.

I never do.

The girl returns with the food, breaking our silent exchange.

We take everything back down to our seats, and I practically inhale the first hot dog.

"Are you going to chew?"

"I like to deep throat it," I say, which earns me a curious look from the guy sitting on the other side of Callum, and then take another bite. "I'm preparing for tonight, Big Guy."

The woman behind me snorts, and I grin. I love making people uncomfortable. I'll never understand why.

Callum bursts out laughing. "Why don't we just leave now?"

Leave early? Hell no. You never know what can happen in the bottom of the ninth. There have been rallies and strange things happen. I stay until the end, clap, tell them good job if they win or lose, and then go on my merry way.

"I have another dog I need to eat, and we need to stay until the end. It's customary to let the boys know we think they did a good job."

"I hope I never understand your mind, it's a wondrous place."

I smile at him. "It really is. I'm kind of amazing."

"Yes, love, you sure are."

And again, Callum manages to make me go all gooey inside. I really hope he knocks that shit off.

"So tell me, how do you feel about me now?"

He looks at me, clearly confused as to what I'm asking. But we've spent enough time together now that I'm curious if he still believes I'm as great now that I'm not a new and shiny toy.

"Feel about you?"

"Yes, do you feel the same or different? I told you I'd ask about your time machine."

Recognition of the conversation we had at the pizza place dawns on him. His hand lifts, brushing against my cheek. "I'm pretty sure you've stolen my heart, Nicole. I'm also sure I don't want it back."

My heart races and my throat goes dry as his eyes bore into me. Damn it. I didn't want to feel this way. I half expected that he'd be bored with me. A small part of me wanted that so I could push my own feelings, that are growing far bigger than I ever wanted, down so I could walk away.

I drop my head, needing to break away from the intensity of his stare. "Let's watch my Yanks kick your ass, okay?"

"Yes, lets. After all, if your team wins . . . I've got another date coming." Callum's grin is victorious.

My mouth opens. "You sneaky bastard!"

He leans over and kisses my neck. "I told you, I don't ever play a game I don't intend to win."

We'll just see about that.

nineteen

. . .

Callum

I HAVE to get back to London.

Not just because my brother is a fucking moron, but also because I need to check on my mum. Contrary to whatever lies she tells herself, she's absolutely getting older. My aunt has been helping out since Milo is "working from the beach," which the bastard has actually been doing, but the point is he needs to be in the office, not out drinking a pint.

I pick up the phone and call the woman who has been my rock.

"Callum." I can hear the smile in her voice. "When are you coming home?"

"I'm not sure, Mum. I have a lot still left to be done."

As true as that is, it is not the entire reason. I'm just smart enough to know saying there's an American love interest will send Mother over the edge. My father was the dark spot on her otherwise bright life.

"Your father was a very organized man, I can't imagine there's much to go through."

"Not when it came to his death," I disagree.

He has directions for everything, but none of it is the way I want to handle things.

"Well, I think you should return to London."

"I'm sure you do. Where is your youngest son?"

She sighs. "Milo is around."

No one loves that man more than my mother. She makes excuses for him, gives him whatever he wants, and has created a damn monster.

"Sure he is, Mum. We both know he took off."

"Give him a break, Callum," she chides.

"Because he doesn't get enough of those?"

I lay my suit out for the meeting I have in a few hours. I'm going to meet Nicole and my lawyers to actually sign the contract. Thankfully, I was able to drag my feet long enough to get her to agree to my terms—an exploration of the relationship we're forming.

"Be nice, Cal. You know losing your father, the one who loved and raised you?" She can't help herself. Any chance, even with him dead, she has to remind me. "It wasn't something Milo ever recovered from. Plus, he thinks you've had it so easy."

Here we go again. I've heard this story a million times, and all I hear is my brother is a numpty. I had nothing easier. Sure, my biological father was loaded and helped me start Dovetail in the UK, but he rode my arse. Nothing was easy or handed to me. It was demanded and earned.

I didn't get to go out fishing with my father on holiday. Nothing was fun about my fucking childhood, but Milo acts as though I was fed from a silver spoon while he ate off the ground. It's bloody ridiculous.

"We'll agree to disagree, but, Mum, I do have to tell you something . . ."

Now to inform her that if my meeting goes well today, I'll be bringing an American home to London for a bit.

"Are there any other loose ends you'd like to discuss?" my lawyer asks as he pulls the contract from his briefcase.

I turn to Nicole. "I do."

"You do?"

"Yes."

Her eyebrows pull in, and I find her utterly adorable. "I want to be sure that once this is signed two things happen." I shift in my chair, but square my shoulders. I have no idea if she'll agree, and if that's the case, then I'll walk from hiring her. I'll pay her whatever she needs to keep her from playing that bullshit card of working for me.

"Okay?"

"I want to be sure what you promised the other night still stands. And I want my second date."

Her jaw drops. "Callum, really?"

"Yes, really. I want to hear it. I'll still sign the papers, but with a broken heart."

She rolls her eyes, mischief dancing in them, and looks at the lawyer. "We slept together, and I told him once this contract was final that was the end of the . . . you know, sex. Then, the bastard coerced me . . ."

"Coerced?" *Please, hardly.* "I don't think it was that way, love."

"Yeah, what do you call refusing to—"

"We get it." I stop her. She really has no issue with speaking her mind.

"Okay, I'm just saying to this fine gentleman that coercion was absolutely what you did. But I said I wasn't going to end things once you and I signed the deal, and I won't."

"Understood." I grin. "Second term."

Nicole leans back with her arms crossed over her chest. "There was only one thing we agreed on, Mr. Huxley."

"I'm aware of that, Ms. Dupree."

"Then there was only one thing and we discussed it."

How wrong she is. "I have another."

"Oh?" She huffs. "I can't wait to hear this."

I have a feeling she really isn't excited, but I need this to work. There's business I need to attend to in London that I can't put off any longer, but I also have a very strong feeling that the minute we're apart, she'll bolt. Therefore, this is the only way I can mitigate the possibilities.

She doesn't know, but the night she invited me to dinner at her friend's place, Heather pulled me aside, told me a bit about Nicole as a teenager. She told me that she was always fearful of being alone. There were times she'd sneak out of her home in the middle of the night, climb into Heather's window, and sleep on the floor. When Heather would wake up, Nicole would explain she was afraid of the silence.

I've seen the hurt and fear that lives inside of her, and all I want is to heal it. Hopefully, we'll heal each other . . .

"I want you to accompany me to London as our second date."

She laughs once. "No."

"Why not?"

I didn't think this would be easy, nothing with her seems to be.

"Because I have a job here."

"You have a company here, I'm now your job."

Nicole's eyes narrow. "Well, technically, I haven't signed anything, *so*." She draws out the last word and gives me a pointed look.

So, she means she doesn't have a job. Walked right into that one.

"You're willing to walk away from the job?"

"I'm saying that you aren't my job."

"No, but I'm asking you . . ."

"No, you're trying to force me," Nicole grumbles.

"I apologize." I touch my chest. "Would you be willing to come to London with me?"

"Why?"

Why is everything a damn fight? That's what I want to yell, but I think about her fears and how hard it was to convince her to let me in a little. Instead of demanding anything, which is what I've always done, I decided to give her the truth. "Because I don't want to be away from you. Because I want to spend as much time as I can with you. I want to show you my life, my job, and I'm hoping it'll be another reason you want to keep me around."

Her lips turn up before I watch her armor slip back into place. "Anything else?"

I've got her now. "Yes, love, because I want you in my bed each night."

She shifts in her seat. "Fine. I'll think about it."

twenty

. . .

Nicole

"GO AWAY, I'M TIRED," I say as Callum shakes me awake.

His deep chuckle fills my ear. "Wake up, love. We're going to land soon."

I haven't done a long flight in forever, and I was slightly worried, but man, this wasn't a normal flight. Callum booked us in first-class—upgraded first-class. We had chairs that became beds with pillowtop memory foam, glass around so no one could see us, and food. Oh, the food. A freaking sundae bar. Seriously, I'm ruined for any other flight I'll ever be on.

Pulling my eye mask off, I stretch. "If I must."

"You must."

"What time is tea with the Queen?" I ask.

Callum huffs. I've asked him this at least ten times, and each excuse has been more entertaining. I can't wait to see what he comes up with next.

"I called and left a message, I'll let you know if she can squeeze us in."

I don't miss his eye roll, and the smile he tries to hide is caught as well. He thinks I'm cute.

"Good. I hope she's ready for this American Princess."

"You're bloody nuts."

"I'm taking that to mean you think I'm beautiful and funny, and you're hopelessly obsessed with me."

Callum shakes his head and then takes my hand. He brings it to his lips, and my heart flutters. "I think I proved that many times, Nicole. I'm clearly unable to resist you."

As if he's the only one. I smile despite myself. "Well, I'm on a plane, so I think that says enough right there."

He smiles. "All a part of my plan, love."

I think about the other night, remembering a small part of what he said about why he calls me love. I really thought I was dreaming, until I realized I totally wasn't. The thing is, from the moment I met Callum, I knew there was something about him. More than the ridiculously good looks and confidence that oozes over him like warm chocolate on a cold scoop of ice cream.

My entire world seemed to light up in a way that I haven't had since . . . him.

It was like I wanted to run to him even though I didn't know him.

And now, I'm following him to the other side of the Atlantic because the idea of being away from him made me sad.

Sure, he had to work for it, but really, that was going to happen anyway. I'm not going to give in that easily.

"Do we have a plan or are we winging it?" I ask.

He shrugs. "I have some plans."

I wiggle my brows. "Dirty ones, I hope."

"Always."

"Well." I lean in and give him a kiss on his lips. "Those are always my favorite kind."

"Mine too."

And this is why I could fall in love with this man so easily.

"This isn't the palace!" I say as we stand in front of Buckingham Palace. It's . . . so not . . . what I was expecting.

"It really is," Callum says.

"It's . . . small!"

He looks at me as if I've lost my mind. "Small? What bloody world do you live in that you think that"—he points to the building—"is small?"

"Dude, it's not even tall!" I huff with disappointment. I've been dreaming of this large castle that was going to make me fall on my design-envy knees. This is not it. It's pretty, and what not, but if I had passed it without the gate, I would have thought it was just a building.

"I didn't know that tall was part of the requirements for a palace."

"Where's the turret? Or the moat! And that's the balcony that Diana waved from? It looked so much bigger on television!" I humph.

Callum rolls his eyes. "You're ridiculous."

"We know this, but you still like me." I wrap my arms around his middle as he chuckles.

"I do. Very much so." Callum kisses the top of my head, and I couldn't care less about the palace or anything else.

All day he's taken me around London, showing me little things, explaining customs and history. This city is amazing. There are so many shops, and the architecture is impossible not to be obsessed with.

"Good. Now, show me where I can find Harry Potter."

"You need to stop watching these movies and shows." Callum laughs, and we start walking.

"Please, I want to go back and tell Finn that I got into Hogwarts!"

Kristin's son is the biggest Harry Potter fan. He's read all the books and has watched the movies multiple times. I'm the cool aunt in this group, so I let him fill me in on all the things over and over again and even manage to tell him some stuff he didn't know. I'm not above hunting down cool facts so I can keep my title. I also take him to Harry Potter World since I'm all about bribery.

Those kids are my version of children. Since I don't plan to have any anytime soon, I spoil the shit out of them and laugh when their parents bitch.

Callum pulls me to his side. "I promise, there's no Harry Potter."

"Way to crush a girl's dreams."

"I'll let you play with my wand," he promises.

"Oh, is it magical?"

"Well, it grows."

"And it shoots things out of its tip."

Callum stops walking and lets out a booming laugh. "Just when I think you can't be any more perfect for me."

I grin. "I'm perfect in general."

"That you are."

I love a man who thinks I'm great. Really, it's the best thing ever. All the guys I've dated before didn't care much about making me laugh or smile. Then again, I never agreed to do a damn thing more than casual with them.

With Callum, I find things are just easy. It doesn't take effort to be in . . . whatever this is. We're compatible, and in the last few weeks, I've done more with him in my life than any other man in years.

The fact that he met my quad says it all.

They're more important than my family.

And they fucking love him. I swear, Kristin told me that if we break up, they get him in the separation and I'm on my own.

Some friends those bitches are.

"You know what else I am?" I ask. "Dead on my feet. How much more walking? I need a nap—and sex. Preferably in that order."

"You have to stay awake. Trust me, you don't want to sleep."

"I want to sleep with you," I say as my hand inches up his chest.

"I promise we'll have a lot of that, but for now, keeping you up and moving is the only way to get through the time change."

"Killjoy."

"You'll thank me tomorrow."

Even though I slept on the plane, jet lag is a real thing. It's only six at night here and I feel like I can't do another two hours, but Callum refuses to let me sit long enough for even a power nap.

"I don't think that'll happen," I tell him. "I'm sleepy."

He stops, brings his mouth to mine, and holds me there. His lips coax mine to open and he slides in. Am I tired? I'm not sure because all I want right now is to curl into him. His hands slide down my back, pulling me tighter against his chest.

I don't care that we're in the middle of some street in London or that closing my eyes feels so good because this feels better. His lips on mine give me a burst of energy I so desperately need.

Callum pulls back too soon. "Now, let's keep walking so I can do that again in a few hours."

"Not fair."

"Neither is you looking the way you do and having to keep my hands off you, but we all have to suffer."

"Oh, you'll suffer later."

"As will you, love."

We start to walk down the street, and I rest my head on his arm. Partly because I want to be close to him, the other is that it takes a lot of energy to keep my head up.

When we get to the building in front of me, I stop with my jaw slack. "Wow." I sigh. My hand hits his chest. "Now that should be the palace!"

"That's Westminster Abbey," Callum informs me.

"It sure is. It's magnificent. It's regal and definitely what I expected Buckingham Palace to be like."

"I assure you, the palace is immensely large. There is nothing spared when it comes to the royal family. They have rooms for days. What it lacks in height, it makes up for in depth. Also, there are several castles that they use, all different architecture."

"Whatever. It should at least have a moat," I state again. "What the hell is the point of a palace without a moat? I really see none."

"It's a palace, not a castle, love. I'm sure the castles they own have moats."

"Semantics."

"Come on." He pulls me forward.

Everything is so beautiful. The stone, gold, and the intricate details make everything look like it was meant to be there. This is so pretty that it's magical.

Callum shows me around, pointing out things that have taken place here, and I'm in awe. I don't know that I actually even understand what he's saying because I can't focus on anything. It's so much all at once, and I want to take it all in.

"This is gorgeous," I say as I keep looking around.

"Yes, it is." His voice is thick with emotion.

I turn to see what he's looking at, but his eyes are on me. "What is?"

He shakes his head. "You."

He's so damn sweet. Why does he have to be so perfect? What flaw am I going to find that's going to remind me not to let my feelings keep getting deeper? Something has to be there because . . . he's going to fuck me up. I know it.

Men like him aren't meant for forever. Men who are this amazing have to have a fatal flaw—it's the damn nature of things. Callum is the answer to every prayer I've ever sent, but he could also bring the darkness if he leaves.

"Stop being so wonderful," I say as a request.

"I'm not wonderful."

"No, you really are."

"Maybe I'm just what you need," he says and touches my cheek.

"Or you could be the one who drags me under."

His thumb brushes my lip. "I don't want to drag you under."

I look up into his blue eyes and hold on to his wrist. "Then don't ever lie to me."

"I won't."

And I believe him. With everything inside me, I believe he'll try his damnedest to never hurt me or lie to me. Every day that we spend together, my heart becomes more and more entwined with his. The vines are wrapping around each other, tying knots, growing stronger, and becoming stronger together than they would be apart.

If I hadn't come with him, I would've regretted it, and I don't ever want to feel that way again.

I rest my other hand on his chest. "I'm done here."

"You are?"

I nod. "Take me back to your place. I have something else in mind to keep me awake."

He smiles and practically drags me out of the church.

Yeah, I'm totally going to hell, but what a ride it will be.

twenty-one

. . .

Callum

I WANT to show her the world. Everywhere we go and everything we do has her face lighting up. I've lived here most of my life, and nothing is ever impressive, but seeing it through Nicole's eyes has made me fall in love with London all over again.

And in love with her.

That fact has me rather tied up inside. It's fast and definitely stupid to let my feelings get so deep so fast, but I'm not a young lad. I know what love is. I've had it, held it, tasted it, and lost it. With her, it's even stronger than I've felt before. If it isn't love, then it's something more, and I'm not willing to let go of it.

"Callum!" Nicole calls me over with her hand waving.

My God, she's beautiful.

I'm a pitiful sap.

This morning, she demanded I take her to the Tower of London, not that she had to demand very hard—I'd already bought tickets. She couldn't stop talking about the Tudors and Anne losing her head in this place.

If I had to listen to her talk about how hot the one actor was any longer, I might have lost my mind, so I agreed quickly.

Now, we're standing here, and every detail excites her. The floods, the Beefeaters, the fact that there are actual homes here, and . . . the beheadings. She really loves that it was a thing.

"Look!" She squeals at the glass monument. "This is where Henry ordered his wife to have her head chopped off. How cool is that?"

"Cool? I'm quite worried about your fascination with this."

"It's your heritage."

I roll my eyes. "I'm not of royal blood. So, it really is not my heritage. Besides, you have capital punishment in America."

Nicole laughs once. "Yeah, they get some drugs and go to sleep! So not the same. You guys were savage. Making them stay up in that tower to look at where they were going to go to die. Seriously, there was some psychological foreplay there. Then you'd march them down from the tower and make them look out at a crowd."

"You know this from experience?"

"Shh." She puts her hand up. "I saw it on the Tudors. Then you'd make them kneel, and—" she makes a choking noise while slicing her finger across her neck. "Head. Gone."

Now I'm truly worried.

"You're very lucky that you weren't around during these times," I tell her as I step closer. The urge to touch her is always strong, but when her guard is down, it's impossible to resist. My arms wrap around her back so I can pull her tight to my chest.

"Yeah? Why is that?"

"Well, if you were around, men would be lining up to court you. I'd be finding ways to get them away so I could be your suitor."

"I would be a commoner. Even worse—a foreigner." She gasps.

"Never. They'd find a way to make you of royal blood. No one as beautiful as you would ever be a commoner."

"Awww, you like me."

"I more than like you."

I would tell her I love her, but I know that will put her over the edge. With her, I feel that exercising my patience is necessary.

"Well, I more than like you." She leans up and kisses me.

I'm not sure that we're saying the same thing, but maybe we are. Only one way to find out. "I want you to meet my family. My mum specifically."

"Why?"

"Why the hell not?"

She shakes her head with a smile. "No, I'm not saying you shouldn't, I'm asking why you'd want to. We're still new."

"Yes, and I had to coerce you to even be here, don't remind me of how difficult you are."

"Charming."

I smirk. "I've charmed the pants off you already."

Nicole bursts out laughing. "I can't deny that. Still . . ." She sighs. "I'm curious as to why you want me to meet your family."

How do I explain it without sounding like an idiot? "Do you not want to meet them?"

"I do."

"And why is that?" I'll turn the tables on her.

"I see what you're doing." Her eyes illuminate as she bites her lower lip.

"What am I doing?"

"Using your charms again."

That is always part of my plan with her. Not because it's an act but because being around her makes me happy. She's funny, unbelievably sexy, smart . . . a perfect match for me in every way.

On top of all of that, Nicole understands the demands of running a company.

When I spoke of needing to work a little last night, she smiled, grabbed her e-reader, and sat on the couch beside me. There was no nagging or complaining about needing time and being a priority.

I love that she isn't afraid to speak her mind. Sometimes, it isn't always appropriate, but she doesn't care, she is who she is.

That's attractive in every way.

"If I was really trying to be charming"—I brush her hair back— "I would tell you it's because my feelings for you are far deeper than you're probably ready to hear. I would say it's because I plan to keep you around for a long time and meeting my family is quite important. But I'm not trying to be charming, so I'll say it's because you're here and why not."

She lifts up on her toes, giving me another quick kiss. "If you were being charming, which, as you say, you're not, I would think that was sweet."

"You would?"

Nicole shrugs as if she really doesn't care. "Well, it's better than saying something like you wanted to have me meet her so you could behead me."

"Seriously, love, there are other things held at the Tower of London."

Her face brightens. "You mean Anne Boleyn's head is *here*?"

"I have no bloody idea. I was talking about the Crown Jewels."

"Oh! I love diamonds."

I'm not at all surprised. I don't know a woman alive who doesn't love jewels. "How about we move on to that?"

She nods. "And we'll find out if her head is here?"

Dear God. "If that will make you happy."

Nicole wraps her arms around my waist as we start to walk. "You make me happy."

I kiss the top of her head. "I'm glad."

I exit the shower and grab my phone. I have two missed calls that I refuse to deal with now. Making my way to the bedroom, I towel my hair and stop when my eyes find her.

Nicole is lying on her side, blonde hair spilling around her, and I swear, each time I see her, she takes my breath away.

I climb in behind her, sliding my arm under her head as she scoots closer to me.

Nicole rolls over, her blue eyes find mine. "Hi."

"Go back to sleep," I tell her.

Her hands touch my bare chest. "I love your body."

"Do you now?"

She nods. "I do. So much so that I'd really like to feel a bit more."

"No one is stopping you."

Her fingertips slide up to my neck and then she trails them down my torso slowly—painstakingly slowly. "I think, this is my favorite part," she says as she grips my cock.

"I can tell you that it likes you very much, love."

Very fucking much.

I move to my back, pulling her on top of me. "Kiss me," I command.

Nicole does as I ask. Her lips are on mine, and it's as if we go from a playful burn to a raging inferno in seconds. She does this to me, drives me mad with a simple kiss. I want to take her, own her, ensure she never forgets who is touching her.

I don't want just tonight, I want every tomorrow.

The thought alone scares me, but then her tongue slides against mine, and I no longer care.

"Why does it feel so good with you?" she asks.

"Because it's how it's meant to be."

She moans, and then our mouths are rather busy again. I cup her arse—one of my favourite parts of her—and slide my cock against her pussy.

"God! It's like it's better each time."

That's because it has been. Each time I'm with her, I find something new that she likes.

I rock back again, forcing her to whimper. "You like that?" I ask as she makes the sound again that I store mentally, ensuring I'll do it again. I love when she can't help but arch her back after I lick around her ear.

Little things that, when combined, will make a big impact.

I roll us both over so I can press against her. My mouth moves down her chest, pulling her nipple into my mouth and sucking hard. I flick the tip as her hands tangle in my hair. "Yes!" She moans.

"I want to hear you," I tell her.

"Make me scream."

I do the same to her other breast, wanting to drive her to the edge, but not over it yet. I plan to be doing something else for that.

I snake my hand between us, finding her clit and rubbing it as I suck on her breast. Each time she squirms, I stop.

"Don't tease me," she begs.

There's not a chance in hell that will be happening. I want to taste her. I slide down her perfect body, spreading those long legs and loving the sigh she makes.

"Let's see if we can get the neighbors to bang on the walls, shall we?" I say before I bring my tongue to her swollen clit.

"Yes!" She calls out as I go to work.

A man should love this as much as the woman he's pleasing. I know I do. While the pleasure I derive is different, it still feels fantastic giving her more than she can handle. Nicole arches her back as I continue to make various shapes against her.

I push faster, sliding two fingers inside and damn near losing control when I feel her start to grip me.

I want her to come around my cock, not my fingers.

Instead of pushing her higher, I stop.

"What the—" she asks, but I flip her onto her stomach.

Quickly, I pull her arse up and sink into her. "Fuck!" I roar.

"You feel so good," she says.

I push deeper, loving the feel of her heat. My hand slaps her ass, and she screams.

"Yes! Callum!"

I knew she liked it rough. I do it again, and she clamps down on my cock.

"Fuck!" she screams as she comes apart. Nicole bucks her hips back as her face hits the pillow. I watch in awe as she releases and continue to ride her.

"That's it, love."

I slide out, putting her on her back so I can see her face. The feel of her around me is no less amazing when I enter her again.

"I don't want this to end," Nicole says.

"It doesn't have to."

"I mean us . . ."

"It's not going to," I promise. "I'm not letting you go anytime soon."

She smiles and touches my cheek. "Are we crazy?"

I kiss her lips, trying to gather my thoughts. Just this morning, I wondered the same thing. If I am crazy for feeling the way I do or if we are just aware of what this is because it is right. If Nicole were to walk away right now, I would be lost. It's crazy, but it's true.

My feelings for her may not make sense, but they're real.

I want to take her to Italy, France, Greece, and anywhere else she wants to go.

I want to give her anything she wants.

I want to show her that nothing else matters but us.

I know what the answer to her question is.

"The only thing that would be crazy is to ignore whatever this is."

Her fingers brush against the scruff on my face. "Then let's not be crazy."

"Let's not."

We don't say another word as the mood shifts into something much softer. The passion doesn't ebb between us. It just becomes what neither of us are willing to admit yet . . . love.

twenty-two

. . .

Nicole

"NO, you don't even understand, Danni. His house is insane!" I tell her as I creep around. "He's making me go meet his mom today, which is crazy because . . . I don't do mothers. Then he wants me to meet his brother, who I saw a picture of, and holy shitballs, he's hot."

"So you thought going through his shit was the way to build a solid relationship?"

"Shut up."

Callum is passed out, and I'm wide the hell awake, so I decided to investigate. Last night was intense between us, and I know my friends think I'm nuts, but there's only one way to find out the skeletons in someone's closets . . . open all the doors.

You think someone is normal until you find a doll head collection.

If I'm really falling in love with him, it's better to figure this out now.

God, I can't even believe I'm using the L-word at all.

"I'm just wondering because you're not known for being brilliant, and this is clearly why . . . he's nice, treats you well, takes you across the ocean, and how do you repay him? By snooping."

"You were my last choice on who to call, just so you know," I tell her as I move to the bathroom area.

"I'll be sure to thank Heather and Kristin for avoiding your call. God knows there's nothing I love doing more than this," Danielle says, and I snort.

"You're my accomplice, be helpful."

"I feel like I'm aiding and abetting," she says as I go to another room.

"Whatever. I'm in another country, you're fine."

"Even better, we're breaking international laws."

I roll my eyes. "Do you have any fun in your life? I bet you're straight vanilla in bed. Do you let Peter put it in your butt? Or maybe he likes it in his butt! Strap-on, perhaps?"

She huffs. "Did you find anything?"

And mission accomplished. Say anything to make her uncomfortable, and I win.

"Nope, which is what has me sure there's something I'm missing. No women's underwear, no strange medications, hell, I can't even find porn! What ridiculously sexy man doesn't have a porn stash? I totally took him for threesome type stuff or maybe even a little male on male *if you know what I mean*," I say quieter than the first part. If he wakes up, I'd like that not to be what he hears.

Danielle goes silent.

"Hello?" I ask after a few seconds.

"I'm wondering where we all went wrong when we friended you . . ."

"Me?"

"Dude, you're insane. You're creeping in the house of a man who flew your ass—first class, no less—to London. Plus, what the hell is the matter with you? You want to find porn or something?"

I huff. "It would at least be normal. What single guy doesn't have porn, Danni?"

"I don't know, Nic, but this is beyond stupid. You have a nice guy there who clearly has deep feelings for you."

I'm aware of that. "I also have . . . nope . . . not saying it. I have nothing but the desire to find out whatever he's hiding."

"You know, you're a real dumbass."

"You're a bitch."

She laughs. "No shit, but at least I'm smart. Tell me that you don't care about him and that's why you *want* to find something."

"I want to hang up this phone."

"Then do it. It won't change the fact that you care about him. If you didn't, you wouldn't be trying to find some trivial thing that would make him dumpable."

My friends are dead to me. Well, at least Danielle is. How dare she be able to read my intentions from that far away. It has nothing to do with her or my feelings. It has to do with not being blindsided.

"Whatever. I'm ignoring you."

"Okay. Well, when you wake up from being an idiot, say thank you, enjoy the sex, admit your feelings are more than the crap you tell yourself, and allow yourself to just go with it."

She's failing to get the point. I don't *want* to admit anything. I want to live in denial because it's nice here. No one gets hurt. No one has their feelings all mangled because one person is a lying asshole. Although, clearly, my heart is already not listening.

"I am enjoying the sex, thanks."

"Out of that entire little tirade, that is what you take away."

"You said sex. I stopped listening after that."

She snorts. "You're a man. I'm convinced."

Wouldn't be the first time they've accused me of being more male than female. "Look, if Peter was doing you the way that I get done, you'd love sex as much as I do. Don't be jealous of my amazing sex life."

"Nicole," Danielle snaps. "I love you, but I'm going to hang up now. I have to get some sleep before I have to get up to get Ava and Parker to school. I'm seriously falling asleep. As fun as this has been, you need to find another friend who has insomnia. I love you."

Danielle is known for always being late because the woman never sleeps. Maybe she's part vampire? Not the scary kind, though, the ones who drink animal blood because they have morals.

However, right now, I don't care about her issues. I'm too busy trying to find out if he collects some creepy weird thing . . . like dolls.

"You're on your cell phone, I can travel with you."

"Oh my God!"

"Get in the car, I need plausible deniability as to why I'm in different rooms."

"I hope he throws your ass out."

"You're grumpy," I say as I open a drawer.

"No, I have my period. I've had cramps, bloating, and—" I close the drawer and stand there counting. The math has my heart racing and my head spinning. She keeps talking, but I can't focus because I met Callum almost two months ago, and haven't had a period since then. In fact, I'm about two weeks late.

"Nicole?" Danielle's voice is animated. "Hello?"

"Shh," I tell her.

"What the hell did you find?"

I start to shake. "Danielle, I'm late."

"You're late for . . ."

My eyes lift, and I look into the mirror. "No, I'm *late*. As in . . . I'm two weeks late."

"Oh." She goes quiet.

"Yeah . . . I've never been late before . . . except one time."

The one time I found out I was pregnant.

"Are you feeling all right?" Callum asks.

I've been quiet all morning. Ever since my revelation on possibly being pregnant, I can't think straight. I'm in a foreign country, yes, it's England, but it's still foreign. I don't exactly think there are any CVS Pharmacies around here.

"I'm not sure." I go with the truth. I don't want to say anything because . . . I'm freaking late for the second time in my life. It could be nerves, flying, stress, or any other craziness.

A few times without a condom could be nothing . . . or it could be the fucking wrench in my life that I'm so not prepared for.

"What's wrong?" The concern in his voice warms me. "Are you worried about meeting my mother?"

Well, now I am. "Just a lot on my mind."

I need to know. I can't wait. Now that it's in my head, it's like a snowball that keeps rolling, growing in size.

"I think I need something for my stomach. Do you have anywhere we can go?"

"Of course." He gets to his feet. "We'll go to the chemist."

I tilt my head. "A chemist? What is he going to do, turn me into some kind of chemical mixture?"

"What? Oh, right, you call them pharmacists." He snorts.

I nod. Usually, I'd make some smart-ass remark, but I don't have it in me at the moment. Just like I hopefully don't have a baby in me either.

"I'm sorry."

"Nicole?" He stands before me. "Are you sure you're all right?"

I get to my feet and place both hands on his chest. "I will be. Can we go now?"

"Of course."

We walk together to the nearest pharmacy, and Callum is quiet, probably assessing my sudden weirdness. I'm trying to be normal, but I'm terrified. Not that I don't want kids, I do, but not like this. I want to be married first, have this grand thing, and then plan for a kid. Maybe even adopt because ... I'm up there in age.

And while my feelings for Callum are strong, I'm not sure that we'll last. Truth be told, I'm shocked I haven't run already.

"Can you give me a few?" I ask him, needing to do this on my own.

"If you would prefer," he offers.

He looks disappointed so I lean up and kiss his cheek. "Thank you."

"I won't lie, I'm rather worried."

I need to pull my shit together. For all I know, I'm going to pee on this stupid stick and find out there's no baby and I wasted a perfectly good morning where I could've been preparing to meet his mother and brother.

"Please don't be. I promise that I'll be fine."

"I'll just be over there." He points to the cash register area.

Great, now I have to find a way to pay for this without him noticing. This should be super easy ...

"Okay."

I head to the back where most stores keep the things no one wants anyone to see them buy and stop in front of a damn wall of boxes claiming to give the earliest results.

Why are there a million brands of pregnancy tests? It really shouldn't be a shop-around type of item. It's a stick that tells you your fate. Also, the technology part of it confuses me. One line or two. Words or no words. Do you want the early detection? It's really not that damn difficult, so why should buying the actual test be? I scan the shelves and pick the one with the best color combinations. It seems like a legit decision, and the longer I stay back here, the more chance I have of being found.

I grab a few things of antacids, some weird-looking bottle that I'm assuming is Pepto, and try to hide the tests inside the shit.

Sure enough, Callum is right there. "You find everything?"

"I did."

"Okay." The worry is clear on his face.

I'm glad I never went into acting. I really suck at it.

"I'll just be a few minutes." I smile at him, praying it doesn't look mangled.

Callum leans in and kisses my forehead. "I take it you don't want me to see what you had to get?"

Fucking hell, did he see me? Shit. Okay, we're grown-ups, and if I'm pregnant, we're going to have to figure things out. Maybe I should get it over with and tell him.

He clears his throat. "I figure you don't want me to see, so it must be that time or something?"

Oh, well, that's kind of a part of it. "Yeah, I mean, we've just started dating . . ."

"Yes, but I don't plan on it being the end anytime soon. I'm well aware of what it's like to have a relationship with a woman."

"Okay . . . so, you must understand I need a little privacy too?"

He nods. "Sure."

I start to walk toward the cashier and turn toward him. "I have to pee real quick too, so I'll be a few."

"There aren't bathrooms here . . ."

What? No bathrooms in the store? What kind of fuckery is this? "Okay . . ."

"There's a Starbucks right next door. How about you pay, and I'll go grab us coffee?"

He's seriously perfect. "That would be great. Thank you."

Callum kisses my forehead. "I'll meet you over there."

I'm grateful he offered this because I couldn't handle another few hours. I have to know if I'm pregnant . . . before I meet his mother.

twenty-three

. . .

Nicole

PLEASE DON'T BE *two lines. Please don't be two lines.*

I'm pacing around the bathroom of the coffee shop, trying not to puke. It can't be positive. There's no way that it will be. I'm smart and take my pill at the same time every single day. I never miss. I'm not on any medications, and we don't need to use a condom with that, right? I'm stupid. I always use condoms. It's a damn rule for a reason. But there I was a horny fucking nut job and practically shoved his dick into me. Well, then again the other night, but I wouldn't be pregnant from that.

I grab my phone and text Danielle.

Me: I'm taking a test.

When she doesn't respond in exactly two seconds, I fire off another one.

Me: You know, to see if I'm fucking knocked up.

Still no response.

Me: You suck as a friend. I'm over here freaking out, and you're ignoring me.

Me: Seriously, I peed on a stick . . . alone . . . and you can't even respond to a damn text message?

Danielle: Dude, it's six in the morning!

Me: And?

Danielle: Jesus, you're worse than my kids. What did the test say?

My stomach flips because I know I should look. I've been in here a while, and Callum is probably out there wondering what the hell is taking me so long.

Me: I haven't looked.

Danielle: Well, look.

I take a deep breath and grab the directions, which I've read seven thousand six hundred and twelve times, just to be sure I don't mess it up. The one window should have a line, and if I'm pregnant, the second window will have a plus. If I'm not, it'll be blank.

Got it.

I grab the test and . . .

What the fuck?

The one box has the line so it worked and the other side has only one line, not a plus, but half a plus. Does that mean I'm half pregnant?

Danielle: Hello?

Me: The test is fucking broken! It's goddamn defective!

I take a photo of the directions and the test and send it to her.

Danielle: Ha! Only you! Okay, you need to take another one in a few days. You're either pregnant but it's too soon or you got a faulty test.

Me: No shit those are my options! I hate everyone.

I let out a huge groan and a few more after it to cover the curse words I'd like to use. Such bullshit. I can't believe this. Of all the damn things not to work, it has to be a pregnancy test. Fuck my life.

Before I can type another text, there's a bang on the door. "One minute!" I yell, pulling out the second test that came in the box.

"Nicole? Is everything all right?"

Shit.

"Yeah, baby. I'm fine. I just . . . my stomach. Gimme one minute." Did I just call him baby?

Dear God, I'm projecting. Also, I don't like terms of endearment. I like Callum, not babe, honey, sweetheart, or baby. He's fucking Callum. The God with a magical penis. If he's getting any nickname, it's going to be Mighty Dick.

Although, he might like that.

"Okay. Are you getting ill?"

"No, I'm okay."

"Are you sure?"

I roll my eyes. "Yes. I'm sure."

There's no way I can spend another five minutes in here, and I don't have to freaking pee again anyway. I swear, my life should be a sitcom.

I slip test number two into my bag of things I don't need, toss the defective test into the trash can, and gather the rest of my self-respect off the floor.

Time to go out there and . . . be a grown-up—and also lie to his face about what I was doing in here.

He's right there when I open the door. "Hi."

"Hello," he says with a raised brow.

"Sorry, you know, girl stuff. But I'm fine now."

He nods. "I was worried."

"No need to be." I give him a sweet smile.

"If you say so . . ." Callum rubs the back of his head, and I see the concern in his eyes. He's so damn sweet. "Listen, I got a call from the office. I need to pop in there. I won't be long."

"Oh! I'd love to come see it," I say with excitement. I've

pictured his office to be very much like his apartment. Callum in my head should be in dark, sleek designs. More slate and steel than mahogany and leather. I can't wait to see if I'm right.

"I'm just going to be there for a few minutes. Since your stomach is bothering you so much, let's get you settled and then I'll bring you by the office later."

I played up the stomach thing and now that's going to bite me in the ass. "I'm feeling much better. I really don't mind."

"Nicole, you've been in there for damn near twenty minutes."

It was not. Ten minutes tops. It took me a few minutes to work up the courage to open the pregnancy test, and then I had performance anxiety, which I now fully understand. If it ever happens to Callum, I'll be nice about it. Then there was the whole peeing and having a broken test.

"Exaggerating much?" I say playfully.

"I got a call from my mother, canceling us going there, then got a call from work—"

"Wait," I say. "We're not meeting your mother?"

He shakes his head. "I'm afraid not."

"Oh," I say, feeling a little miffed.

Why am I disappointed? I hate mothers. All of them. They're nosey, judgmental, and often remind me that I'm not good enough for either their precious son or anything else. Meeting her wasn't what I wanted, but I wanted to share something with him. Know him on a deeper level and maybe get to see some embarrassing pictures that I can use against him later.

She was the one who wanted to meet me in the first place, so it makes no sense now why we aren't going. "Why did it get cancelled?"

He runs his hand down his face. "Mum was invited to visit a friend who has been sick for quite some time. She wants to see her while she can. Hopefully, we can catch up with her tomorrow."

Oh. Okay. I mean . . . it makes sense. "Sure, that's fine."

"Good. Let's head back to my flat, you can lie down while I sign a few documents and then we'll head out and do something if you're up to it."

"But I'm up to it now."

"So you weren't sick in there? I heard you grunt and groan like you were in pain. I was damn near ready to break the door down."

"No, it was just . . . nothing."

"I'd still feel much better if you rested so we can go out tonight."

I'm not used to being babied, but he's being really sweet and I'm not telling him the whole truth. "Okay, I mean, if it'll make you feel better, even though I'm completely fine."

Just freaking out a little on the inside.

Although . . .

If he leaves me alone in the apartment, I can take the second pregnancy test without him there.

This might be okay.

twenty-four

. . .

Nicole

IT'S BEEN ALMOST two hours.

I'm definitely pregnant and alone, so each minute that ticks by is torture. I'm so messed up I can't even tell my friends.

All I've done is talk myself in circles, trying to figure out how the hell this happened.

Unlike the first test, the second didn't do the half-plus, not-really-all-there thing, nope, this one was a bright pink positive.

I can't think. I can't wrap my head around how. Ninety-nine percent fucking effective my ass.

I get up and start pacing again. I need to tell him, but how? Do I just be, like, hey, Cal, guess what? I'm having our love child? Or do I wait until after I see a doctor and have it confirmed? You'd think that, at my age, this wouldn't be a concern, but here I am ... concerned as fuck.

Instead of doing this mental breakdown ridiculousness, I could call one of my friends, but ... I won't.

Callum should be the first person to know.

Then, together, we can come up with a plan, because right now ... I got nothing.

I grab my phone and check the time . . . again.

Two more minutes gone.

I need to do something—anything. So I text him.

Me: Hey, where are you? I'm going stir crazy here.

Callum: I'm on my way. It took a bit longer than I hoped.

No shit. Long enough for me to find out we're having a baby and to lose my shit.

Me: Okay. See you soon.

Callum: I miss you.

Awww, he's so sweet.

Me: I miss you too.

And I do. Not because I just don't want to be alone here but because I found myself wanting to snuggle into him.

Jesus, I'm officially one of my stupid lovesick friends. Someone needs to slap me.

I decide I literally can't take the silence and being alone, so I video call Heather.

"Hey!" she says with a huge smile. "How are you? How is London?"

I want to tell her. She's been my best friend, and we really don't keep secrets from each other, but I know the right thing to do is to talk to him first. Like a couple would do. "I'm okay," I say and then switch right away. "London is amazing. We went all over. It's nothing like I remember in college."

She laughs. "Well, I don't remember much about college. Way too much beer."

"Very true. How is Eli? Are you guys in Tampa now or somewhere else?"

Heather has been traveling with her husband because the idea of being away from him makes her nuts. She was the most independent person I knew, but when her sister passed, something changed inside her.

I don't know if it's Eli, grief, or that she hates her job. Being a police officer is hard for her, mostly because her ex-husband is her boss. That isn't awkward at all. Matt, Heather's ex, and Scott, Kristin's ex, could form a club for douchebags with little dicks. I'm not sure who would be the president of it . . . maybe they could do a shortest-straw-wins competition? Either way, they both suck.

We celebrated both their divorces.

"No." Heather's lips turn down. "He's in L.A. for a few days. I'm headed into work because I can't seem to quit. Brody cries when he has to ride with another partner."

"When is your next shift?"

"In about an hour."

"Callum had to run to the office," I say, and she laughs. "Why are you laughing?"

"Dude, your face. You looked like someone took your favorite toy away."

"I like his toy."

She rolls her eyes. "Yes, we know, you like to play with all the sticks."

"You can say dicks, Heather. It's totally allowed."

"I'll remember that. When are you coming back home?"

That's the million-dollar question. I've been here for a little over a week, and Callum hasn't mentioned anything other than a quick trip somewhere before we head back to the states. No idea what the hell he has planned, but I'm not complaining.

Since I've been here, my creative juices have been pumping into overdrive. I don't know if it's the details in all the buildings or what, but I have so many ideas.

"We haven't gotten there yet, but I'll let you know," I promise.

"Okay. You look really happy, Nic."

I smile. "I feel it. I don't know. He's so great, and so many things are happening with us . . . really fast. It's scary, but I'm happy."

Heather's eyes are filled with warmth. "I know that you have this secret that you don't think I know."

Oh, fuck.

She continues on. "I've let you have it because I know you need it. Kristin didn't tell me either, so you can put that out of your mind. Just remember what I do for a living. Anyway, whatever happened with you before is in the past. You were the biggest Eli advocate I know. You pushed me and Kristin to open ourselves to whatever was coming, and I'm asking you to do the same."

I lean back against the headboard. "I'm pretty sure I already have."

"How so?"

"As scared as I am . . . and I'm fucking terrified," I admit, "I really like him. I could love him."

"Could or do?" My face falls, and she shrugs. "Please, you're the most annoying ass I know. You don't give us any room to get out of things, welcome to the other side."

"Whatever."

There's a buzzer going off behind her. "I have to get to work. I love you!"

"I love you too."

"You do and you love Callum! Bye!"

And then the bitch hangs up before I can say anything else.

Callum should be home any minute. Maybe I should take a shower? I can let the steam calm me, and I might be able to get my brain to settle down. Sure, like that ever works.

Standing in front of the mirror, I place my hand on my belly. "So, I guess you're in there," I say to the baby. "I'm your mom. I'm also a hot mess, and your dad and I aren't married, but you know, I'm the least traditional person in the world. I'm pretty sure I'm going to suck pretty bad at this because I'm . . . a mess. I've done things that I can only pray you'll never do. Although, I'm sure you will since you're half me."

It's best to establish that honesty is the best policy early, right?

"Okay, so, whatever happens, just know that I'll be trying really hard not to fuck you or this up. I can't make promises that I won't, little baby, but I will do better than my parents did. That's not really a great measuring stick, but it's all I got."

I look at myself for another few seconds and then I hear a door.

Oh, God. He's home.

Jesus.

Okay, I need to stay calm. My heart is racing, and my stomach is filled with lead. I don't know how he's going to react, and I'm afraid.

Callum has never shown me any sign that he'd be cruel in any way, but . . . this is a big deal. This is a *baby*.

There are real things here to consider. We're really new, and he may not want to be hitched to my wagon forever, but with a kid—he will be. It's also going to be a shock because this never should've happened. It did, and even if he gets mad and doesn't want to be obligated to this baby or me, I wouldn't take it back. I can do this on my own. I'm financially stable, and for the most part, mature enough. Whether Callum wants to be in the baby's life or not, I can do this.

I've helped raise—corrupt—my friends' kids. I know how to change diapers, and I'm sure they'll be there to help. Whatever his reaction is, I'll be fine.

Now that I've worked that all out, it's time to go deliver the news.

I head out to the living room, only he isn't there.

"Hello? Callum?" I call out.

"Hello," a woman with long dark hair and brown eyes says. "Who are you?"

Maybe this is his cleaning lady? "Who are you?"

"I'm Elizabeth Huxley."

I've never heard that name before, but it still has my pulse spiking to insane levels. "Callum didn't mention anyone would be coming over."

Please, God, be a sister or cousin.

"I see. I'm not surprised since he tends to leave important details out. Who are you?"

Déjà vu hits me so hard I can't breathe. No. Not again. No. I can't.

"I'm Nicole."

Elizabeth looks me up and down with a harsh look. "Well, Nicole, if you could get your things and leave my home, I'd appreciate it."

"Your home?"

Please don't say the words that I know are coming next.

"Yes. I'm Callum's wife, and this is my flat."

And the floor drops out from beneath me.

Again.

I've done it again.

twenty-five

. . .

Callum

THE TRAFFIC IS HORRENDOUS. What should've been a twenty-minute ride has taken me over an hour. I've sent several text messages to Nicole, all have gone unanswered.

I park, grab the box sitting on the passenger seat, and head up to my flat, waving to the doorman on the way in. I'm anxious to check on Nicole. Hopefully, she's gotten some rest and will be chuffed about what I have planned.

The reason I didn't want her to come to the office was because of what's inside here. My assistant has been working non-stop to get this trip right. In a few hours, we'll be on a plane to Tuscany. We'll spend the next week going to various vineyards, restaurants, and staying in the lushest hotels I could find.

I want to spoil her, make sure that everything exceeds her dreams.

When I get to the door, my phone rings.

"Yes, Milo," I answer.

"I hear you're going to Italy for a week."

"You heard right."

He laughs. "Now who is chasing a woman?"

Idiot. "I own the company, there is the difference, brother."

"Oh, is that how it is? Well, I'm not sure what you summoned me for earlier. I'm dealing with some . . ." I hear him whisper to someone. ". . . important things."

"I asked you to come to the office so I could inform you of the changes happening at Dovetail."

This isn't the way I want to tell my brother. My assistant, Margaret, had assured me that Milo confirmed he would come to the office. After an hour of waiting, we finally got word that he was . . . indisposed.

That was the final straw.

"What changes?"

Here goes the fun part. "I'm going to move to America in the next few months."

"You're what?" he yells into the receiver. "Are you fucking mad? What do you mean move to America?"

"It's really not that difficult to understand, Milo. The company is merging with the London office. We'll be under one corporation, and it makes more sense for me to be the CEO and work out of the office there."

"Then who is going to run the London office?"

He will never forgive me for this, but I have to make the right business decision. Milo is my brother, and I love the bastard, but I'm tired of his antics. I need someone I can trust and who will do what's best for Dovetail, and that person isn't him. The sad thing is that it's not like Milo is incapable of handling things. He's brilliant, but a numpty.

"Edward."

"Edward! Fuck you, Cal!"

"Don't be mad at me for your poor decisions. You wanted to go roam the bloody world, here's your chance. If you piss Edward off, he'll fire you."

I can hear him breathing loudly through the receiver. "I can't believe you. You're my brother, for fuck's sake!"

"Yes, I am your brother, and because of that, I've put up with your shit. However, I'm not going to let you run my company into the ground. I need someone I can trust and who will actually show up to work."

I grip the back of my neck and rest my head on the wall. I hate this. I hate it more than I can say. My mum is livid and is refusing to speak to me, which is part of why she cancelled. She will get over this, but my brother won't.

"You really feel that way?"

"Do you think I like this, Milo? I am taking no pleasure in promoting Edward over you. I wanted you to be my right hand. I begged you to stop being so bloody selfish, but even now, this is about you! Not what's best for Dovetail."

He scoffs. "You think Edward is? The man is incompetent!"

"No. I thought you would be. You're smarter than anyone else who works for the company, but you think with your cock, and that doesn't work for me."

"Well, now I don't either. Piss off," Milo yells and then disconnects the phone.

Jesus Christ. At least on the other side of this door is someone who actually still likes me.

I turn the knob and what I find . . . is definitely not who I am hoping to see.

"Elizabeth, what the fuck are you doing here?" I glare at the woman I despise more than anything.

"Hello to you too, Cal."

"Get out." I point to the door.

"Now," she purrs as she gets to her feet, "is that any way to speak to your wife?"

"*Ex*-wife."

"Oh, whatever. We'll forever be married in the eyes of the Lord."

I laugh. "I'm pretty sure you're going to hell, where all demons belong. We're divorced, I framed the damn paperwork to commemorate the day I was done with you."

Elizabeth Webb was a beauty. She was everything a man could want. Breathtaking, smart, could handle any dinner situation, and came from money so there was never a worry about being used. I thought she was the sun until I realized all that lived in her was darkness.

She is conniving, manipulative, and has no problem sleeping with anyone who catches her damn eye.

For years I thought that, if I could just make her happier, she'd finally stop.

She didn't.

I divorced her five years ago, and yet, she still finds ways to make me miserable.

"You were always so dramatic, much like your new girlfriend. Such a pity she ran off in such a hurry."

"Fuck!" I roar. "What did you do? Why are you such a bitch?"

"I just told her about our marriage, which apparently you failed to do."

What is wrong with her? "You're fucking insane! We're not married. I don't think what we had was ever a marriage. Where is she?"

"How would I know?" She shakes her head with an eye roll.

I stomp forward, trying to rein in the fury that threatens to overspill. "You have taken everything I care about and ruined it. Get the fuck out of my home and out of my life, Lizzy, before I do something I will really regret."

I don't care about Elizabeth. That ship sank years ago. What I do care about is Nicole, and my ex-cow of a wife has made her think we are married.

"Don't be ridiculous," she tsks.

"What did you say to her?"

"Nothing she shouldn't have already known. And really, Cal, an American? I'm sure your mum is chuffed about that."

I throw open the door. "Get the fuck out."

"I will as soon as I tell you what I came for."

My heart is racing, and my mouth tastes metallic from the adrenaline. I have to find Nicole. I have to explain because God only knows what Lizzy told her, and I have to make this right. "I don't give a damn about anything you have to say."

"Well, you'll be interested when I tell you I plan to sell my shares of Dovetail."

Those ten shares and seat at the board are going to haunt me the rest of my life. However, right now, I don't give a shit. She has no idea I now own the American company, which is exactly what I need. She's always thought I was too sentimental, that I didn't think with my brain enough and with my heart too much. Maybe she was right at that time. Now, I'm not the same man. I have plans for those ten shares, and Elizabeth is playing right into my hands.

"Do whatever you want, Elizabeth. I've had enough games. I need to find my girlfriend and fix the mess you've made."

She walks over, and her pointer finger touches my arm, which has me jerking back. "I almost forgot." She sighs. "She left you a note in the kitchen."

Then the bitch walks out.

twenty-six

. . .

Nicole

CAN you dehydrate from crying too much? If you can, I'm pretty sure I'm on my way there because I can't stop crying like a lunatic. When the looks got to be overwhelming, I spent a good ten minutes in the bathroom of the airplane sobbing. I'm sure people thought I was insane, but I don't care.

After Elizabeth filled me in on everything I didn't know, I threw whatever I could grab into my bag and got a ride to the airport. On my way, I found a flight leaving in three hours and secured a seat to go home.

They upgraded me to first class—thanks to my breakdown at the counter about being pregnant and finding out the baby's father was married to someone else. Not my finest moment.

Now, I'm standing in the Tampa airport, feeling completely lost.

My phone rings, and Kristin's name flashes across my screen.

"Kris," I say. Once again, my friend will deal with the fallout of my bad choices. Once again, Kristin is who I will lean on because she has the kindest heart. She won't make me feel worse than I feel already.

"Nic, you need to come home." Why does her voice sound as broken as mine does?

"I'm . . . I'm at the airport . . . in Tampa."

"Oh! Okay. Look, I have to tell you something." Kristin sniffles, and even with as devastated and broken as I am, something in my gut says there's something seriously wrong.

"What's going on?"

"How quickly can you get to my house?"

"I'll get a ride now. Is everything okay?"

She hiccups. "No, just get here. It's . . . it's Danielle."

I pick up the pace, no longer focusing on myself. "Is she okay?"

"She's fine, but it's Peter . . . just get here. Ava and Parker are with me, and I could use your help."

"I'm on my way."

My heart is racing as I try to get to the baggage claim area. I don't know what's going on, but if she called me because she needed me to come home, it must be bad.

I rush to get my bag off the carousel and grab a cab.

On the drive to Kristin's, the sadness that I'd pushed aside moments ago starts to creep back in. Last week, I was in a car going to the airport with Callum. I was filled with so much hope and excitement, but now I'm broken.

I fell in love with Callum, only to find out he wasn't mine to love.

Now, I'm pregnant and have to figure out what all this means. He knows I left. Has probably read the note.

Fucking asshole.

It wasn't like I had much to say to him, but I'd put money on my words being more than enough to get my point across.

Fucking liar. Met your wife. I'm pregnant and hate you.

. . .

We pass his apartment building, and I flip it off. I'm so angry. I'm so hurt. I'm so mad at myself for thinking that he was different and that we had something special.

I trusted him, and then his wife shows up . . .

I just . . . I still can't believe it.

"Miss?" The driver calls my attention, glancing between the rearview mirror and the house we are stopped in front of.

"Oh. Sorry." I hand him the money and when I slide from the car, Kristin is standing on the porch.

One look tells me that something is most definitely wrong.

"Hey," she says as I approach, and my heart begins to race.

"What's wrong?"

"It's so bad, Nic. Danni is a mess and on her way here now to tell the kids. Peter was shot."

"Oh my God!" I gasp. "Is he okay?"

She shakes her head. "No, he was killed."

My lips part, and I clutch my chest. "No," I breathe the word. Peter isn't my favorite person, he never has been, but Danielle loves him. They have those two beautiful kids, and he made her happy.

"I know." Kristin's lip trembles. "Noah is in with the kids now, but . . . this is . . ."

"Horrible." I finish her sentence.

My life may be in shambles, but my best friend's world was obliterated.

Kristin looks to the house and then back to me. "Those kids . . ."

"Ava is going to be a wreck."

Peter is Ava's whole world. That girl loves her father more than anything.

"It's good you're here. She's always been super close with you."

Kristin is right, Ava is my girl. She comes to me about everything. When she first liked a boy, she told me about it. When she wanted to know about shaving her legs, I was the one to sit on the tub with her and show her how. Hell, I bought her a bra when her mother was in denial about the girl having boobs.

"I can't believe this."

She nods. "Why are you here?"

Now is not the time to get into it. "I'll tell you later."

"No." She puts her hands on her hips, her eyes flitting between my red-rimmed eyes and my splotchy cheeks. "Something is wrong. Tell me now."

I shake my head, knowing that if I start, if I admit this all aloud, that I won't be able to stop the tidal wave of pain that will come.

"Please . . . just let me focus on Danielle. She's going to need us, and so is Ava. I can't do that if I let this out."

Kristin's eyes narrow, and there's a flash of understanding. "Okay, but you'll tell me later?"

I nod. "I don't think I have a choice, do I?"

"No. Not really."

A moment later, Danielle's car pulls up. Heather is driving.

Kristin and I walk over, and the look on Danielle's face breaks me. I know that look. I'm feeling that same loss right now. It's knowing that everything you thought you knew was a lie. It's pain so deep you feel as though your bones are about to shatter. I can feel the pain in her chest. Her tears are my tears because the four of us share something special.

Our friendship has gone through so many tests and has never faltered.

This will be another thing we get through—together.

As soon as she's out of the car, the four of us embrace. Danielle cries, and we all let go with her.

"He's gone! He's gone, and I'm alone. He's dead. He won't ever walk back through the door."

"I know." Kristin rubs her back.

"He's gone, and I have to tell the kids."

"We're all here for them," I assure her.

Tears spill down Danielle's face. "Make it stop. Make it not be real, *please!*" she begs.

I wish I could do that for her. Seeing my friends suffer is worse than any pain I could endure. She doesn't deserve to have this happen. Danielle has a huge heart, and she's loved Peter since she was in college. No matter what they've gone through, he's the only man she's ever loved.

I brush her hair back, my own tears mingling with my friends. "We can't. But God, we wish we could," I tell her.

Danielle starts to go limp, but we hold her tightly. "How do I tell them? How do I tell the kids their father was shot and killed? They didn't know he wouldn't come home tonight." She sobs. "They didn't say goodbye like they should've. None of us did. I would've told him . . ."

All of us look to each other with our own tears. There're no words of comfort we can offer her, just support. "He knew," Kristin tells her. "He knew you loved him."

Danielle's eyes are void and hopeless. "Did he? Because I did a really shitty job of telling him." She releases a heavy breath and straightens. "I don't know how I'm going to get through this."

Heather pulls her into her arms. "You'll do it because you have three people right here who love you and who will hold you up. You're never alone. You're never without an army beside you, ready to help fight your wars." She looks at me, and even though she doesn't know a thing, I feel like the words are for me too. "We have your back. We will never let you fall."

"Ava . . ."

"I'll be here for Ava, and so will Heather and Kristin." I touch her arm. "Don't worry, we'll help her."

Heather nods. "Remember, I've been there too. I lost my

parents and sister. I know how hard this is, but we'll do whatever we can."

Danielle takes my hand, and for the next few hours, I forget that less than a day ago, my life was great. I put aside the fact that I can barely breathe without my chest hurting, and I do what I can to ease someone else's pain. Because that's what you do when you love someone. You don't lie. You don't hurt. You heal.

twenty-seven

. . .

Nicole

DANIELLE and the kids have gone home to be with their families while Heather, Kristin, and I sit in Kristin's living room.

It's been an intense few hours, and I'm physically and emotionally exhausted.

"You guys okay?" Heather asks. "I'm really tired and today was a day I'd like to wash off me and go to bed."

Kristin and I get to our feet. "You should go," she tells her. "I don't know how you dealt with all that."

Heather was one of the police officers to arrive at the scene. She saw it all and had to be the one to tell Danielle. She puts on a good show about being strong, but I think she's reached her breaking point.

"I did what any of us would do."

No, I wouldn't have been able to do that. To know that the words I spoke to our closest friend would forever alter her life. She's so much stronger than she even realizes.

I pull her into my arms. "Is Eli home?"

She nods. "He texted me that he's there."

"Good."

Her husband has this sixth sense when it comes to her.

"Let us know you got home okay?" Kristin, the perpetual worrier, asks.

"I will. I love you guys."

"We love you too," I tell her.

We all walk to the door together, and Heather turns quickly. "How did you get back from London so fast?"

I guess I was lucky enough to have avoided the cop in her for as long as I had. I knew it would have been too good to be true to get away with it completely.

"Callum and I are over."

"What?" Heather practically yells. "No! Why? Why are you such an idiot? He's so good for you!"

Good for me? Please. "Why is it me? Huh? Why is it something that *I* did? What about him? And no, Heather, he is *not* good for me. He's fucking married!"

My lips start to tremble, and a tear forms. Fucking Callum. I'm crying again.

"Nicole?" Kristin's eyes fill with worry.

"Oh, and I'm pregnant."

"You're what?" Heather gasps. "Oh my God, Nic." She quickly gathers me into her arms as I cry harder. "I'm so sorry. I didn't know."

I don't want to be comforted. I'm angry, hurt, and unbelievably heartbroken. I tried so hard to deny my feelings and act as if things were okay, but they aren't. I'm not. None of this is even remotely okay.

"I'm pregnant and . . . oh, God, Callum's wife came home early from wherever she was, I guess."

Kristin's hand covers her mouth. "Jesus Christ. Did she say anything?"

Did she ever.

Elizabeth didn't hold back.

"She told me to get my shit out of her home, and . . . I fucking hate him. He lied to me."

Kristin pulls me from Heather's arms and into her own, holding me tight as I do what I never do . . . I break down. I cry so hard that my chest actually hurts. Speaking the truth has broken the last barrier I had. She rubs my back and Heather comes around, enveloping us both.

"It's okay, Nic."

"No, it's not!" I start to sob. "None of this is okay!"

Heather pushes my hair back to look at me. "Okay, it's not. What did he say when you told him you found out?"

I move back, wiping the stupid tears that won't stop. "Nothing. I left! What can he possibly say that would make a difference? His *wife* said it all."

Kristin chews her lip and then brushes my arm. "You know, I don't know Callum well, but I can tell you that I've been on the other side of this. I don't know if I would've had the balls to march in to see what I was in denial about."

"Yeah, but I would have," I counter.

I would want to catch them and then I would make their lives hell. If I gave my heart to someone, like I did Callum, and he trampled it after we were married, you're damn right I'd be guns blazing.

I didn't this time because he wasn't mine. He was never mine.

"True, but what I guess I should say is that I've also been in a situation where not everything was quite as it appeared . . ."

She's talking about what broke her and Noah up for a period of time. "That was different. You're a good person."

"And Callum isn't?"

"I don't know what Callum is other than a liar! He didn't want me to go to his office, why? He didn't want me to meet his mother or, at least, he said she had to cancel, yeah right. Then his wife shows up, spewing all her shit . . . so, yeah, I don't think that's the makings of a good person, do you?"

What is she not getting? I know that Kristin sees the good in people and situations, but there's nothing here that can be prettied up. He lied, he cheated, and then the fucker got caught.

"Okay, what did the wife say?" Heather questions.

"She told me who she was, and then she told me to get my shit and get out."

"And you left? You? Of all the people in this world, you let someone order you around?" Heather's eyes are filled with confusion.

"Yes, because she said they've been married for eight years and that Callum has been cheating on her practically the entire time. They've been trying to work things out, and it was great until his father died and he went to the States."

"That makes no sense," Kristin says.

"What part?"

"That they were working things out and then his father dying starting him back to cheating again. Doesn't he hate his father? Also, Callum practically twisted your arm to get you to go to London with him, why? If he knew there was a chance of his wife finding you at his place, why would he? Why would he want you to meet his mom? It doesn't make sense," Heather finishes for her.

"Maybe she wasn't supposed to be there?"

"Has he shown you any indication that he would be hiding something?"

Jesus, why are these two so quick to find a flaw in this. "Kristin, you of all people know why this would be the fucking worst case scenario for me."

"I know. What about the baby?"

I look down at my stomach. "I'll be a single mom."

"Are you going to tell him?"

The note I left did. "I'm sure he knows by now."

"Are you okay with having a baby?" Heather asks.

That's the sad thing. I am actually a little happy in some weird part of my brain. I love Callum. I know that it would have been hard, but we would've figured out how to be great parents. Maybe I would've moved to London. Maybe he would've come to America to be with us. Maybe the fucking white horse would've grown wings to carry our new love that we were feeling to Neverland. That possibility was burned to ashes as soon as I heard the word *wife*. Even with as much as I hate him, I could never hate this baby.

"I never thought I would, but . . . I mean . . . I'll figure it out, right? You guys will help since I'll be doing it alone."

Heather and Kristin share a look and then Heather starts again. "You need to retract your claws for a minute and hear me out . . . can you do that?"

"I'm not sure," I tell her the *truth*, which is clearly a concept Callum has no knowledge of.

"Try," Kristin urges.

"Fine."

Heather begins. "We know that you've been hurt. I know you've shared your story with Kristin, and I'm glad, but I'm going to guess . . . you were with someone before, and it turned out he was married. You thought he was a good man, and even in all your crazy ass ways, you'd never knowingly sleep with a married man. Am I right?"

"Yes."

Shame hits me. It was a long time ago, but I still feel it. I hated myself for years. I felt as if punishing myself was the only way to atone for the destruction I caused that family.

"Okay, did you know he was married?"

"No!"

"Then you were not the person to blame," Heather assures me.

"No, you weren't." Kristin smiles as she shakes her head. "I

don't know the situation with Callum, but I can tell you this . . .
when a wife finds her husband cheating, she doesn't just stroll in,
hoping to find her husband in a compromising position. I never
wanted to see or even know about Scott and Jillian. I will also say
that you should've talked to him. I've been on the other end of a
miscommunication, and had Noah and I just talked, it would've
been okay. Instead, he left angry, and it turned out to be a mess."

I remember that whole thing since she came to my house.
This? It is totally different. There aren't many ways you can
misconstrue meeting someone's wife.

"What possible miscommunication is there for being
married?"

Heather shrugs. "I'm not sure, but I read people for a living,
and there was nothing I picked up on with Callum. But put all
that aside, you're having a baby, and he does need to be a part of
the equation. You should probably talk to him."

"I'll talk to him when I can string words together and not cry. I
will never let a man see me cry like that again."

"Fair enough." She nods.

"Besides," Kristin calls our attention, "you have three million
reasons you should call him anyway."

I groan while looking up at the sky. "Fuck. I hate him so
much."

Kristin sighs. "No, you love him, and right now, you're in pain,
but you're a professional and can handle this."

This is why I never sleep with clients. There's nothing more
awkward than having to deal with someone after you've fucked
them until you've blacked out and are carrying their love child.

twenty-eight

. . .

Callum

I STAND OUTSIDE HER FLAT, knowing this conversation will make or break us. I looked for her, tried to call her, waited at my home, but she never came back. Then I realized that she left, left. Like got on a flight and went home.

Now, I'm standing here, hoping she'll hear me out.

I spent hours on the plane, restless to get to her, knowing the more time that passed, the worse this will be. My ex-wife is a cunt, and I'd like nothing more than to bury her, but as they say, only the good die young. Elizabeth will live forever at this rate.

I'm not sure what it is that she refuses to let go of. We had a loveless marriage. She was too busy trying to find new lovers and spending my money to love anyone but herself.

Sitting on the floor of the hallway, I have nothing to do other than think and plan. Of course, nothing sounds good enough or like it isn't a load of bullshit. It is going to be impossible to get her to hear me out, but I have to.

Then I think about her note. When I read the words, my heart stopped.

She's pregnant.

"What are you doing here?" Nicole's voice is filled with a mix of sadness and anger.

I pop to my feet. "I'm not married."

She shakes her head. "I've heard that one before."

"I swear it."

"Your word means nothing to me, Callum."

I hate that she sees it that way. Her eyes pool with tears, and I take a step forward. "Don't cry."

"I'm not! It's the goddamn hormones! You don't get to make me cry anymore."

"I never wanted to make you cry at all."

"Well, too late for that." She digs around in her purse for her keys. "Go away."

"No."

The guilt for being the reason she looks sad is eating away at me. Nicole is normally so bright and warm, and I've broken that. Right now, she's angry, hurt, and distant. I need to fix it.

I'm not leaving. She has to know the truth and know that I will do anything to make this right. I'm a bloody fool for not telling her to begin with, but nothing was done with malicious intent.

"God, you're such an asshole. Did my avoiding your calls and texts not send a clear enough message? We're done. I'm a mess, and you made me that way."

She isn't a mess. She's beautiful.

I take a second to look at her and even with her red, puffy eyes, she's the most gorgeous creature I've ever seen. Her blonde hair is pulled back, and she's dressed in a pair of sweatpants and off-the-shoulder top. I wouldn't change one single thing.

"I'm the one who is fucked up. I should've told you about Lizzie, but I couldn't admit it."

"Please, just stop. If this is about the baby, I won't be that girl. You can see him or her anytime, and we'll work it out."

"That won't work for me," I tell her.

I'm not walking away from her. Baby or not, I love her. I want a life with her, and I'm not going to lose her because of this. I can't endure it. The last three days have been absolute hell. I had to get things in London settled, and the moment I could, I was on a plane to America.

Nicole takes a step back. "I'm not asking you."

"I love you, Nicole."

She laughs. "Are you fucking kidding?"

"No."

"You know, I actually fell for it all over again," she says with disbelief. "I thought you were different. I thought that even though all the things I was feeling were so intense and quick, it was because this was right. I thought I could love again." Nicole puts her key into the lock, and I know I'm losing her. "I thought I could be healed because what we had seemed like a fairy tale. Then I find out that not only it is *not* a fairy tale but also I'm the villain in the story."

She opens the door and steps through. I know this is the last chance I have. My hand stops the door before she shuts me out and closes the door on us.

"You're not the villain, and this is exactly the story we were in. I'm divorced. I left Elizabeth six years ago after her . . . God only knows what number affair she had. Our divorce was final five years ago." I take out the paperwork to prove it and hand it to her. "Read it. It's all there. I never lied to you. I didn't tell you because that part of my life died. She was dead to me, and my marriage was a sham from day one. I don't even consider her a part of my life. It was painful for me to admit that I was a failure at being a husband. If I had known . . ."

Nicole grabs the paper from me and looks at it. "Thanks for clearing that up," she says and then shuts the door.

I guess I have more groveling to do.

twenty-nine

. . .

Nicole

THE PHONE RINGS AGAIN.

I glance at the screen, see Callum's name, and send that shit right to voice mail.

It's been a day since he was here, and I still refuse to answer any of his calls, return his texts, or read any of his emails. He's resorted to calling my assistant, who is doing a bang-up job of ignoring him.

There is nothing he can say at this point that I want to hear. In my head, he kept something from me, which is as bad as a damn lie. He didn't tell me about her or that he had been married. Had I known she existed, when she showed up, I could've handled her.

Instead, I had to stand there and feel like complete shit.

Sure, I get that he's divorced, which is great, but he could have offered up the information when I asked him if he was married. He chose not to.

I'm sitting in the doctor's office, waiting to go in, when my phone rings again. I don't even look before putting the phone on silent.

Take a damn hint, Callum.

My OBGYN wanted me to come in right away and have the pregnancy confirmed. Since I've miscarried in the past and am the ripe age of thirty-nine, they want to be cautious. Peter's funeral is tomorrow, so I figured I should get checked today. Plus, it's another way to avoid Callum.

I'm being a bitch, I know this, but I'm hurt.

I'm also scared out of my mind because if I let him start explaining things, I'll cave. If I cave and something else happens, I won't ever be able to make it through losing him again.

These last few days have been hell. I've never cried so much.

I really built up this fantasy in my mind, and when my history repeated right in front of me, it was torture.

"Are you not going to forgive him?" Kristin asks from the chair beside me.

"You're still here?"

She rolls her eyes. "You can pretend I'm not, but yes, I'm here. Ass."

Kristin refused to let me do this alone. She should be with Danielle, but she said I needed a friend more than anyone.

"To answer your question, I'm not sure."

"He didn't lie."

"Yes, yes he did."

Kristin shrugs. "I think you're trying to go into self-preservation mode."

I think my friends are far too nosey for their own good, and I'm well aware of what I'm doing. It's called surviving, which is the same damn thing as self-preservation.

"Can we focus on the fact that I'm knocked up?"

"We could, but you're knocked up by a guy who flew over here to fix shit with you, gave you proof that he isn't married, and has explained that his ex-wife is apparently Jillian's long-lost cousin from hell, and you *still* won't take the man's calls."

"So, you're going to be silent?" I ask.

"Not a chance."

"You used to be my favorite," I tell her.

"I'll live with the disappointment."

I love Kristin. No matter what, she's always hovering at that top spot. She's like a damn panda bear, you just want to hug her. "I can't stay mad at you. Which makes me hate you more."

Her hand covers mine. "I know. It's part of my charm. Back to Callum . . ."

So much for charm. "Why are you pushing this so hard?"

"Because he didn't do anything, and now you're using some lame-ass excuse to walk away from him. Had you stayed and talked to him, you wouldn't be such a nutjob."

Like any of these bitches can talk about being crazy? No. Heather is a lunatic, Kristin is a nut, and Danielle is . . . well, she's allowed to be whatever she wants to be. I'm the only sane person in this group.

"I wouldn't talk."

"You know what? You're right," she says and sighs.

"Huh?"

"You're right."

Why do I feel like this is a trap? One that I'm going to hate myself for walking right into? I feel like this is one of those Mom tricks where the kid ends up agreeing to something they know they didn't want to do just because they got talked in circles. The woman is trying to use some Jedi mind game on me to get her way.

"Good," I say hesitantly. "I think . . ."

"I'm serious. It's a good thing that you're going to walk away before you love him. It hurts so much more after you get *those* feelings, you know?"

Here we go.

Kristin continues. "It's best to lock your heart up, throw away the key, and be a single mom instead of being with a man who clearly loves you. I would totally do the same. Smart on your part."

"Just stop," I beg.

"What?" She gives me her most innocent expression. As if I would believe that shit for one second. "I'm agreeing with you."

"So, if this were Scott—"

"You can't even remotely compare what Scott did to what Callum did," Kristin silences me. "Scott was my husband and did cheat. He lied, and put me down until I believed I didn't deserve anything other than what he was giving me. Callum may have withheld information, but he isn't actually married and, from what you have told me, he's done everything to make you a better version of yourself. Oh, and the man is fighting for you."

"I'm fighting for peace and quiet," I moan.

"Too bad. Welcome to life with you as a friend."

Am I really this annoying? Jesus, I want to slap myself. Then again, if it weren't for me pushing my friends to get their heads out of their asses, I would be dealing with the calls, whining, and all that. At least now, their husbands, boyfriends, or whatever we're calling them these days have to listen to them.

Where is that damn doctor? The best way to shut her up is to get called back there.

"Nicole?" It's a voice that I never wanted to hear again, and I turn to Kristin, who looks every bit as shocked as I feel.

"No." I try to look away, pretending it isn't me. I can't handle much more.

"Nic?" Kristin whispers, her eyes flashing over my shoulder before coming back to me.

I can feel the color drain from my face. This can't be happening.

"It's him," I whisper back.

"Him?"

I give her a look, and awareness flashes in her eyes as she puts it together.

Andy walks toward me in his suit. He looks exactly like I remember, only now, he isn't attractive at all. He doesn't have strong arms that will make me feel safe or the consuming presence that seems to follow Callum around. His hair is too light, and the sound of his voice does nothing for me.

"I'm here on a sales call. My company handles all the fetal monitoring equipment for this group . . ."

"I don't care."

He nods. "I figured. Listen, I want to say I'm sorry."

I look up at him as if he's lost his fucking mind. "For what?"

He's a little late to be apologizing.

"Everything. I was a real asshole to you, and I'm sorry."

This is the most ridiculous conversation. I get to my feet, not wanting to make a scene but willing to if it means he goes the fuck away. "I'm just sorry I believed you. If you could please . . ."

"I was lost. I know that's not an excuse, but you made me feel like I was found. I left my wife, by the way, or well, I should say that she left me."

"Good." I snort. "I don't know what you want from me, Andy."

"Nothing. I took enough from you."

I release a heavy breath and close my eyes. For so long, I've waited for this moment. A time to tell him all the things he did to me, how he hurt me, how he broke something inside me, but now that I have the moment, I don't even want to look at him.

"You hurt me. You hurt me in a way I never thought I could be hurt."

"It wasn't my intention."

Like I give a shit. "What did you think was going to happen? You could live with me, stay married, and we'd all just find a way around it?"

Everything inside me is crumbling, my heart, my chest, my

willpower to not lash out at him. I've spent all these years hating myself for what I allowed to happen. There were so many nights where I would lie in bed, wondering how I could be so stupid.

"I know this isn't the answer you want to hear, but at that time, I didn't care. I needed you."

"You needed therapy," I spit. "You were selfish, mean, and irresponsible. You could've made so many different decisions. You know what the worst part was?"

He shakes his head and has enough decency to look contrite.

"That when I lost the baby, I was happy. Hell, I didn't even tell you because I never wanted you to know there was something of us living inside me."

"You were pregnant?"

My hand instinctively covers my stomach.

"Was. I lost that baby because you destroyed anything good in my life."

I think that, right there, is what I struggled with the most. Sure, I cried, but I wasn't *sad*. I was relieved. I didn't want any ties to Andy or that life.

With this baby, I never would've felt that. If I lose this child, I'll never recover. My entire life will cease because I already love him or her. Callum's child. It came from a place of love. It came from two people who were broken thanks to other people . . .

"That's enough, you've said your peace," Kristin says to Andy while touching my back.

"Take care, Nicole."

"Fuck off, Andy."

He walks away, and I want to throw something.

"Well, that should settle that," Kristin says from behind me.

I turn to look at her. "What?"

"You definitely shouldn't work things out with Callum. Nope. Seeing them side by side, you're totally right. He's a bastard just like that one."

I go to open my mouth to defend Callum. He's nothing like Andy. Nothing. But before I can say a word, the nurse calls my name to go back. I turn, but not before seeing the grin on Kristin's smug face.

I'm officially one hundred percent pregnant.

The blood test and ultrasound say so. Though, I'm dubious about the weird-looking balloon thing turning into a child at some point.

Kristin doesn't say a word during the ultrasound. She sat there with giant, silent tears tracking down her cheeks. Then, when I would look at her like I might choke her, she would stop. Who knew that a baby was all it took to shut her up?

Once we get to the car, she finds her voice and keeps talking non-stop. Throughout the drive home, I sit in a fog, wondering what exactly I'm feeling. Seeing Andy was a blow to my defenses.

I'm not sure if forgiving Callum is the right thing for my heart, but I know it's what I want to do deep in my soul. My life is better with him in it. He's made me smile, laugh, and trust, which are things no one else has been able to do.

I love him.

I love him and I hate him at the same time.

"What's going on in your brain?" Kristin asks. "I've been talking, and you haven't said anything."

"I'm thinking."

She laughs. "That's what the burning smell is."

"Fuck off."

"You're totally going to need to watch your language. You've got nine months to curb it before the baby comes."

I roll my eyes. "No, I just need to teach the kid not to say fuck, shit, and all the other crap that comes out of my mouth."

Now she bursts out laughing. "Oh, is that how it works? I didn't know that with two kids and all . . . thanks for that tidbit."

I hate her.

"Whatever. I'm not even going there yet. The only thing I can think about is how the hell I'm going to do this."

"Well, you're going to eat right, take your vitamins, drink lots of water, and continue to grow Callum's . . . I mean, your little miracle inside you."

I narrow my eyes at her because she totally did that on purpose. "I hope you get pregnant."

She glares at me. "Nope. I take my pill like a good girl."

"I took my stupid pill too!"

"Well, mine works. Yours doesn't. Noah and I are content. We're happy not being married or having kids."

I mimic her, saying, "Not being married or having kids."

"Good to see you put your grown-up pants on," Kristin retorts. "Listen, you're going to be fine. You really will. Even if you don't get your head out of your ass and realize you have an amazing man who loves you and deserves to be forgiven for something he didn't even do." Her eyes roll while she shakes her head. "You'll be fine. You're having a *baby*! A baby! Gah!"

She's seriously so optimistic sometimes that it's gross.

We turn into Danielle's neighborhood. We refuse to let her handle funeral arrangements by herself, and there is still stuff to be done before the service tomorrow. I've handled the flowers, transportation, and picked out his headstone, but Heather is helping her make phone calls and arranging the reception afterward.

The good thing is that Peter had really clear instructions on what his wishes were. I just facilitated it all.

"Are you going to tell Danni you are in fact with a bun in the oven?" Kristin asks as I watch the cars pass by.

"Maybe. I don't know. She knew I took the test, but I haven't said anything since then."

"You should."

I should do a lot of things. "I don't want to make her grief about me. She has so much going on that the last thing I want to do is make her think she has to pretend to be happy."

She touches my hand. "No one would ever think that. Besides, maybe we could all do with a little happy in our lives."

"Maybe, but . . . I mean, it's not like it's happy news."

"Stop it. It might not be expected, but it's not bad news. You're going to have a baby, and as your friends, we are happy about it."

And the unicorns are riding in on their clouds from heaven.

When we pull up to Danni's house, my jaw drops. Callum is sitting on her porch step.

"What the hell? Is it cheating husbands who slept with Nicole day?" I ask as I cross my arms, refusing to get out of the car.

"He wasn't married, but I get your sentiment."

I glare at her. "Really?"

"I'll handle him," Kristin says as she gets out of the car.

I sit here with a grin on my face, hoping she gives him hell. She points at his chest a few times, and I imagine her cursing him out, telling him all the ways he was wrong. Sweet, funny, and full-of-hope Kristin's arms go flying in the air, and Callum's head drops.

Yes! Give it to him!

I'm feeling victorious, and I didn't even do anything.

She continues, her hands rising in the air again before flinging out toward where I'm sitting in the car.

"That's it! Tell him how he doesn't deserve to be around me!" I say from behind the window. "Yeah, and you can leave!"

Her shoulders fall, and I clamp my lips shut because . . . no. Just no. When he extends his hand and she takes it, I want to beat against the window. "No, no, no."

He kisses the top of her knuckles, and she tilts her head as her damn shoulder rises like she's this sweet docile girl.

"Damn it! Resist him, Kris," I say, tapping the window. "Hey! Don't fall for it!"

Of course, no one looks in my direction or hears me.

Then she hugs him.

The fucking traitor hugs the bad guy. What in the actual hell is going on? Callum's eyes meet mine, and he grins at me as if he knows I'm next.

That's it. Bastard picked the weak one.

"Asshole," I grit out between clenched teeth and exit the car.

It's time the big girls handle this shit. Apparently, Kristin isn't angry enough. I got that in spades.

I slam the car door and march toward him. "Hey!"

"Love."

"Oh, I'm not your love. What do you want?"

"You," he says in earnest.

"Nope. You had me, but you lost that chance." I cross my arms over my chest.

"Nic—"

I turn to Kristin and scowl. "You should be ashamed of yourself. You said you'd take care of this. What the hell was with you talking to him and then falling for his crap? Seriously, you suck."

"I did handle him. Just not the way you would've."

I roll my eyes. "How? What is it? Hug a Cheater day? No. You were supposed to be all mean and shitty."

"I was mean!" she defends. "But, dude, he freaking loves you so much . . . and let's be real, you're not the easiest person to love. You're kind of a dick."

I'm well aware of that, but that isn't the point.

I face Callum again. "You love me?"

"Yes."

"Too bad!"

"What's going on?" Danielle says from where she's standing in the open doorway.

"Nothing. I'm getting rid of a pest problem," I inform her.

Kristin snorts. "Yes, he's the pest? I don't think so."

Danielle steps out. "Nicole? Why are you yelling at Callum?"

I shake my head. "No reason. Go inside."

"Wait, why were you already back from London when Peter . . . oh my God!" Realization flashes in her eyes. "You're pregnant! Aren't you?"

"Yes, and she won't talk to me," Callum says.

"Because you're a liar, and I thought you were married!"

"But I'm not. I gave you the proof you needed, and you still won't give me a chance to show you that I love you. That you're the only woman I want and need."

Danielle steps closer. "Wait, married? What the hell?"

I look over at my friend. "Danni, you don't need to worry about any of this."

"Why? My husband is dead, he's not coming back to life. My life sucks fucking donkey balls, so at least tell me why you're slightly miserable."

Kristin laughs once, and I level her with a stare.

"Someone needs to fill me in." Danni waves her hand in front of us all.

"Callum was married."

"So?" she asks.

"He never told me about it, and his bitch of an ex-wife showed up at his apartment and told me she wasn't an ex."

Her mouth drops open. "Oh, wow. Yeah, dude, you fucked up."

Callum nods. "Believe me, I understand it was a grave error on my part, but I've tried to explain that I buried that life behind me once my divorce was final."

"Clearly, you haven't if she has a key to your apartment!" I flip him off. "Asshole."

Danielle and Kristin glance at each other and then to Callum.

"She didn't get a key from me! My doorman, who no longer is employed at my flat, gave her a bloody key."

"Stop having answers for everything!" I yell and take a step forward. "You hurt me! I cried like a fucking crazy person on a flight back home!" Another step. "I thought . . . I thought all these things. I felt pain so deep I was convinced I was going to die! Do you get it? I don't do that! I'm the strong one out of these people!" I shove his chest. I hate him so much for making me weak. Something that I haven't allowed anyone to have the power to do in a very long time. "Now you made me just like them!" I point to my friends.

"Umm," Danielle says, but Kristin must've stopped her.

I'm too focused on Callum to see why she didn't finish the thought that probably would have sent me into another rage. "I didn't want to care about you. But there you were, in my stupid heart, ripping it apart. Now you put a damn baby in me!" I push him again. "I hate you!"

Callum grips my arms, pulls me tightly to his chest, and then drops his mouth to mine. He kisses me so hard I can't move. Every muscle in my body is locked as he pushes against my lips. Anger, hurt, and disappointment flow around us, and then he softens just a bit. I kiss the asshole back. I kiss him through all the hurt he caused, the love I feel for him, the confliction that is like a vortex deep inside me. I want to hate him, but no matter how much I try to convince myself I should, I can't.

The truth is, he's the only man I want. He's the only person who has loved me for who I am. He didn't try to change me or make me into someone I'm not. He's the calm to my crazy.

Sure, he didn't tell me about his ex-wife, but he is here. He's here and as much as I wish I didn't—I believe him.

He lifts his mouth from mine, and I stand here like a statue.

"I never wanted to hurt you," he says and then places a soft kiss on my lips. "I never wanted to make you weak." And again he kisses me. "I love you and the baby inside you. I'm going to make this right. I can't endure another day without you. Please forgive me."

One of the two assholes beside me audibly sighs.

As cheesy as his words were, I know what he means. I may be angry, but underneath that is sadness and fear. Each night, I've reached for him. Missed the sounds of his snoring and the feel of his skin. I've longed for him, which is why I've soaked my pillows with tears.

"I don't want to be hurt," I admit. "I don't want to feel pain anymore."

Callum's hands cup my face. "Then don't walk away from me again."

thirty

. . .

Callum

MY HEART IS POUNDING against my chest as I wait for her to say something. I can't and won't think about this failing. I came here, wanting to lend her support. I heard about Peter's death on television and came to pay my respects to Danielle. She thanked me for coming with Nicole. It seemed as if she didn't know that Nicole ended things with me—although, with all she has going on, I can see why. Danielle explained that Nicole and Kristin were on their way, and I asked if I could wait.

I didn't know how it would go over. It's clear Nicole's hurt is deeper than I had thought, but I was determined to show her how good I was for her. I needed to get her to hear me, listen with her heart, and try. Nicole, however, tends to try to speak first.

So, I now have a new way to shut her up a bit—kiss her senseless and then make her listen.

Her eyes show the hesitation that must be in her heart, and I rub my thumb across her cheek, trying to smooth some of it away. "I won't keep things from you again," I promise. "If I hadn't been so dead-set on moving on from the divorce, you would have known about it. I had no idea that would be how you found out, and I'm so bloody sorry. All I want is to make you happy again. Let me back in, love. Let me remind you how good we are."

I see her soften, and my hope grows that she'll see how much I truly love her.

Her hand moves to my chest. "I'm pregnant, Callum."

"I know."

"Is that why you're here? Because of the baby?"

"No." I don't hesitate. "I'm here because of you. I came because losing you isn't an option. I don't care if I lose everything I own, everyone else in my life, anything I care about, as long as I have you. Because it's you." I graze her cheek again. "You are what I care about the most."

"Oh my God, Nicole," Danielle grumbles. "Forgive the man already! Men like him don't come around all the time."

I like her.

Nicole rolls her eyes and loses a deep sigh. "Fine. But if you fuck up again, you're dead to me."

I bring her lips to mine and kiss her before she can change her mind.

Clapping sounds from her two friends, and she smiles against my lips. "I really hate them."

"I don't believe that's true."

She turns to them. "They'll pay for it, I promise."

Danielle waves dismissively and then she and Kristin head inside.

Nicole buries her face against my chest and inhales. "I'm going to be skittish."

My hand moves against her back. "Will you tell me why?"

Slowly, she lifts her head and takes a step back. "I was in love once before you. One time, I let a guy into my heart. One time, I thought that I could do it, I could be like my friends."

I move toward her, not wanting to let her retreat too far.

"Anyway." Nicole tucks her hair behind her ear. "I was naïve or whatever. He was a client, and I was helping him design his office and also an apartment. It turned out that he was married and had a family. There were so many things that I ignored. I wanted so badly to believe that I was just being crazy and it was in my head, right?" She dips her chin, but it only moves a fraction before she's lifting it again. "I was so wrong."

Jesus Christ. No wonder she flipped out and left. It also makes sense why she was so adamant about her rule. "I wasn't lying to you or carrying out some crazy affair."

"But look at it from my standpoint. You were my client, and I have a strict no-fucking-the-client rule. I never wanted any man to have the ability to hurt me again, which you did. We went to London and made all these plans, but then your mom cancels and you didn't want to take me to your office. I was like, am I being crazy or unaware? Then some chick comes in and says she's your wife. What was I supposed to think?"

I take another step closer because I won't let her push me away. She may not realize she's doing it, but each time she speaks, she puts more distance between us. I understand putting up defenses more than she knows.

"None of that should've happened, and that's my fault. Just as you, I've had my head fucked with. Lizzie was my life, I loved her and wanted to make it work, but she was—is—selfish. It's been years since I've dated anyone. I felt no need, until you. I love you, Nicole. I meant that when I said it."

She looks to me with trepidation. "I love you too."

"Then know that my not telling you was really because I've tried very hard to forget. Probably the same reason you never told me about the man who hurt you."

"Stop making sense." She huffs but stops retreating.

"Stop being stubborn and come here."

The challenge is there, she doesn't like being told what to do, but I see how much she is fighting against herself.

"If I do . . . you're going to kiss me," she informs me. "You're also going to have to prove that you love me."

I smile and stand my ground, waiting for her to move toward to me. "I'll do more than that, but you have to come here first."

And then she walks right into my arms, where I plan to keep her.

thirty-one

. . .

Nicole

"ARE YOU ALL RIGHT?" Callum asks as he holds my hand while we drive home.

I can't stop crying. I'm like a damn leaky faucet with the tears. Peter and I may not have seen eye to eye, but watching Danielle in this much pain has been insanely hard. I feel it as though it's my own. Then I think, what if it was Callum?

What if it I lost him?

I know how much it hurt when I thought we were over, but to have spent our lives together, have children, and then to have him taken without warning . . .

And here come more tears.

"It's just so sad."

He nods. "Peter was a good man."

"Yeah, it just makes no sense. I mean, how do you find any kind of peace after that? How do you explain to your children? How do you go on?" I ask rhetorically. "I can't imagine her pain," I sob.

I rest my head on his arm and he kisses the top of my head.

"She's lost the love of her life."

"I don't ever want to lose you," I tell him.

I didn't plan to say the words, but they're out there now.

"You won't."

"You can't promise that. You're not invincible, Callum Huxley."

He smiles. "No, but I will always find my way back to you."

"I appreciate the bullshit, but . . . *God*, I'm so freaking hormonal! I've cried more in three days than I have in the last ten years!"

We get back to my apartment, and I go to reach for the wine, needing a glass more than ever. Damn it. I can't drink.

I already hate this pregnancy. It's making me cry all the fucking time, and now I can't drink.

"Shit!" I yell.

"What is it?"

"Can we have sex?"

Callum starts to take his shirt off. "I'm all for it."

I start to huff and puff walking around the kitchen. "No! You don't get it! I don't know if we're allowed. I mean, what if your big dick hits the baby?"

"As much as I appreciate the compliment. I'm pretty sure people have sex whilst being pregnant. I doubt many couples go nine months without it."

Well, isn't he just so smart? Great, another mood swing. I turn around, slamming my hand on the counter.

"What's wrong, love?" Callum asks while wrapping his arms around me from behind.

"I can't drink."

"That is true."

I look at him from over my shoulder. "It's totally your fault."

"This is also true."

Well, at least he can admit it. I turn around so I'm facing him. There's been so much on my mind, and now that all the wife shit is cleared up, things need to be addressed.

I'm not sure what to do or think, but I've learned that communication is key here. "Can we talk?"

"Of course," Callum says. "What's on your mind?"

"So many things, but mostly . . . we're seriously having a baby."

The look of pride on his face makes me want to slap him and kiss him. Which . . . I might just do.

"What are you worried about? Money?" he asks, and I scoff.

"No. I have money."

"As do I."

"Okay, what about raising him or her? What about custody? What about all of that?"

His arms drop, and he takes a step back. "I assumed we would be doing this together."

I'm not sure what to say to that. Does he mean like a team? Or does he think something more? I'm done making assumptions and accusations. I want us to talk.

"Can you clarify what that looks like?"

"It means we'll get married and be a family."

My lips part, and I take two steps back. Callum, noting my retreat, follows forward. "I need space," I tell him, putting my hand up.

He stops moving. "I need you to stay with me here."

"I'm right here, but you can't be serious. Us having a baby doesn't need to equal marriage."

"I'm aware of that. I don't want to marry you because you're pregnant. I want to marry you because I love you."

"Callum, it's too soon!"

"Says who?"

"Says me, you crazy person!" I shriek.

Marriage? A baby? Is he insane? Yes. Yes, he is. There is no reason we need to get married. If I wasn't pregnant, we wouldn't be having this conversation. No, we'd be in bed and he'd be getting the ride of his life.

Make-up sex is the best sex.

"Why am I crazy? Because I love you and I don't ever want to spend a day apart from you? Because I named a CEO of Dovetail in London so I can be here full time, which I did before you left me because you thought I was married. Because I think about you all the time and wish to have you as my wife?" He takes a black box from his pocket and holds it out to me. "I got this three weeks ago. The day after the baseball game, I walked by this jewelry shop by the pizza place, saw it in the window, and I knew . . . I knew I had to have it for you."

My legs start to quiver, and my throat goes dry. "Callum . . ."

"I planned this grand thing before you took off, you know?"

I shake my head.

"We would've been in Italy right now, going up and down to different vineyards and places. I planned to take you to this fantastic restaurant in Tuscany that has the most magnificent view."

Tears form in my eyes. I know what he's going to do, and I appreciate that he's stalling so I can say the right thing.

"I was going to get down on one knee." I watch as he does what he just described. "I would've taken your hand in mine, like this, and then I would have asked you if you would be my wife. If you'd let me take care of you, love you, and give you the world."

Water leaks from my eyes, but this time they aren't sad tears. "Is that what you're doing now?"

My mind wrestles back and forth between being crazy and just following my heart. I love Callum. I know there's no one else I want. I know that he gets me, accepts me, and is the man I'm meant to be with.

"Yes. I'm asking you if you'll marry me, Nicole Dupree. Be my wife. Not because of any reasons other than I love you more than anything and want to spend my life making you happy."

I smile, knowing there's really no question about what I should say. "On one condition," I put it out there.

"Name it."

I take his face in my hands, and smile. "If you only wear Yankee hats from now on."

Callum chuckles. "I'll be their number one fan."

I bring my lips to his and then nod. "Yes, I'll marry you."

His mouth closes over mine, and he kisses me senseless.

"You know?" I say between kisses. "We're going to have to get married in a few weeks."

"Fine by me." His voice is full of passion as he brings our lips back together.

Which I don't really have a problem with, but I'm serious.

"No, like, we have to get married very quickly."

He grins. "Tomorrow works."

"Cal!" I push him back.

"Nicole, I will marry you tonight if that is what you want."

"You're that sure?"

"I'm that sure."

"So if I said let's get on a plane and get married tonight, you would?"

He nods. "Yes. Is that what you want?"

"No, I want my friends and our families to be there."

His arm tightens and he holds me closer. "Then that's what you'll get."

I really love this man. "Well, okay then."

"Is there anything else, or can I take you to bed now?"

My fingers graze his stubble. "Talk dirty British to me and I'll shut up."

Callum grips my hand, pulling me back to the bedroom. When we get there, he turns, his eyes are hungry, and I like it.

We're going to have naughty Callum tonight.

He lifts my dress, revealing the fact that I've been commando all day.

"Jesus Christ," he groans.

"Well, what are you going to do about it?"

His hands cup my ass, lifting me in the air as he walks back and then places me on the bed. I expect him to get on top of me, but he doesn't. He drops to his knees on the side and his mouth is on me a moment later.

"Yes, right there!" I scream as he's between my legs.

His tongue moves in another circle and then he pushes a digit into me. My walls clamp around his finger, and I grip his hair, holding on as my orgasm comes on fast. When his teeth close along my clit, giving enough pressure—I explode.

Damn this whole pregnancy thing might be a goddamn wonder. I have never gotten off so fast.

Callum's eyes meet mine and the smug grin says he's pretty damn proud.

"I'm going to make love to you, darling," he says.

He removes his clothes and climbs onto the bed. "You really suck at this dirty talk."

"I promise to defile you later, tonight, I need to love you."

I understand what he's saying. We almost lost each other, and I can see how much that hurt him.

"We're going to have a lifetime of love, Callum."

His lips press to mine. "This is one I want you to remember."

My hand slides to his cheek, and the ring on my finger reflects the soft lighting all around us. "I don't think I'll ever forget tonight."

He pulls my hand down, looking at the ring that rests there. "I love this. I love knowing that you've agreed to a life with me."

I smile. "I love you."

"You've truly made me the happiest man in the world."

My eyes glimmer with tears. I cry so easily, whether I'm happy or sad. Stupid hormones are making me a cry baby.

"Stop being sweet." I wipe my face. "I don't like it."

"I'm always sweet."

"Yeah, stop it."

He laughs and then kisses my lips. "Would you rather I be mean?"

My head moves side to side before I bring my mouth to his. "No, I like you sweet, but I like when you're naughty too."

Callum is a match to me in every way. I like him sweet and loving, but we both like to play rough. He's adventurous when I want him to be, and he knows I'm down for just about anything. However, I don't want anyone else to share our bed.

For the first time in a long time, I don't need or want another man to give me what I'm lacking. He's all that I need.

"Tomorrow, love. I'll be as naughty as you like."

"Well, then, let's make love, and then for round two, we can pretend it's after midnight."

"I like how you think," he says as he lines up with my entrance.

"Make love to me, Callum."

He pushes forward, filling me in every way possible.

"Do you know how much you mean to me?" he asks between thrusts.

"As much as you mean to me."

"Not possible."

I grip his face, my eyes telling him everything that's in my heart. However, I say it aloud just so there's no misunderstanding what I'm feeling. I'm going to be so vulnerable, but that's what he deserves, my soul. "I love you with my entire being. I plan to make those vows to you because you are my heart and soul. I know a thousand people will have spoken them before, but no one will have ever felt the way I will saying them. Now, shut up and make me come again, okay?"

"How about I make you come twice for that?"

I grin. "I look forward to you trying."

"Me too, love. Me too."

thirty-two

. . .

Nicole

"YOU REALLY DON'T WANT to do a big wedding?" my mother asks.

"I don't have *time*." I groan. "I'm not wearing a pregnancy wedding dress, so it needs to be soon. Like, less than a month timeframe."

She shakes her head. "I wanted grandkids, I didn't expect it to be out of wedlock."

Now she's worried about customs? "I'm just saying that we're going to do something very lowkey."

"It just doesn't seem your style. You've always been over the top in everything you've done. I expected it would be the same with this since you like to be the center of attention."

Just once I'd like not everything out of her mouth to sound like an insult.

"I'm happy just doing it before the baby comes."

"Had you told me about this two weeks ago when it happened, I could've secured something fast," she scolds.

"It's fine."

"What about the club, Nicole? I can get that."

I would rather swallow nails. "No."

"But you met Callum there."

I glare at her. "I also know that, if we have it at the club, you'll invite a million people."

"Your father will want it to be an event as well. I know you don't care about decorum, but we both have images to maintain. What if I could assure you it'll all be done in less than a month?"

Why is she pushing this so hard? "Mom, it's fine. Callum and I are really good with it just being family and the girls. Besides, it's really pretty much impossible to do a big wedding at this point."

Maybe if I had told her when he asked me two weeks ago it would be different, but I didn't. I didn't want to hear her opinion or tell her I was pregnant. I wanted to just let her and Callum settle into liking each other, which they have.

It would've all gone fine, we were going to elope next week, come home, and tell everyone, but then my stupid ass forgot to take my engagement ring off when I met my mother for lunch. It was downhill from there.

"It is never too late." She pulls her phone out. "Give me forty-eight hours. If I can't get all of it settled by then, you can go and do whatever horrendous version of a shotgun wedding you want. Will you give me that?"

She is not going to let this go. As much as I don't want to agree, there's a part of me that wants to see what she can do. The other thing is that this is my wedding, the only one I ever plan on having. I've been practically designing it since I was twelve.

I've always wanted the big day with thousands of pink roses, tulips, and camellias filling the venue.

I've dreamed of the slip dress that's tighter up top and fuller on the bottom. It would have no back so it's both classy and sexy.

My shoes . . . God, the shoes are so perfect. I have a pair of white lace Christian Louboutin heels that are absolutely the hottest thing ever.

They're the shoes you leave on when you fuck that night because *you* actually want to see them up over his shoulders. Seriously, some stellar shoes.

All of this has been a part of my mind for as long as I can remember, and there is a small part of me that was disappointed that I wouldn't have it.

Of course, the wedding is important, but really, it's the guy who will be waiting for me at the end.

"You have twenty-four hours. And if it's not what I want, then it's not happening, understood?"

Her face lights up. "Don't challenge me, darling. You're about to lose."

Is anyone really losing here?

"Okay, Mom, do your worst."

———————————————

"Did you really think Esther was going to fail?" Heather asks. "That woman is a wrecking ball in a china shop."

"I think the phrase is bull in a china shop."

She rolls her eyes. "Same shit."

I slide the dresses on the racks, trying to find the ugliest one I can. I'm not a nice bride. I'm *the* bride. I want to be the only thing anyone at the wedding looks at. I'm also vain enough to admit it. So, I'm going to be that dick friend who finds the bridesmaid dresses that look like tents.

And then I find a gem. "Here!" I lift it up.

"Are you serious?" Heather's eyes go wide.

"Kristin! Danni!" I call the others over. "I found it!"

They both head over, and Kristin gasps. "What the hell *is* that?"

"Your dress! Isn't it great?"

Danielle still hasn't moved.

"They're something." Kristin damn near gags.

I smile, knowing they hate it. I feel like there are very few things in this world a girl can do to payback her friends. When Danielle got married, we were young and really freaking broke, so we got some weird-ass dresses that she said we could wear again—lie.

Then Heather's first wedding was a theme. A fucking theme. No one, other than her, thought it was cute to make us dress as though we were in some Victorian era with some weird vest thing that smooshed our boobs up into our throats. No one. But we did it. I stood next to her, looking like a total idiot, and smiled.

Kristin was the only one who really didn't make us suffer. She picked out a simple style and let us wear whatever color we wanted. Something about a rainbow symbolizing love or whatever. I feel bad for making her suffer—just kidding, no I don't.

This dress is a mix of a tablecloth and a quilt. It's going to look awful, and I don't care even a bit.

"Hopefully, they'll be able to order them if they're out."

"Oh, yeah, hopefully," Heather says and then makes a horrified face.

Danielle finally speaks. "You're serious? Like this isn't one of those Nicole does some crazy thing, we laugh, and then we move on to the real dress?"

"Nope. I'm dead ass serious."

"Why do you hate us?" Danni asks.

"I don't hate you, babe." My hand grabs her arm. "I just want you to be uglier than me, that's all."

"Oh my fucking God!" Heather yells. "You're an asshole."

"No, I'm the bride. And *you*"—I point my finger at her—"of *all* the people in this group, you get the least amount of say here."

"Me? What the hell did I do?"

"You made us look like fucking milkmaids at your wedding. So you can shut up, smile, and wear whatever shit I pick out."

Danielle and Kristin nod in agreement. "Seriously . . ." Danielle laughs. "I burned that dress in our firepit."

"I was young!"

"And we looked ridiculous!" I yell back.

"It was cute," Heather defends with her arms crossed over her chest.

Danielle snorts. "It was beyond stupid."

We all start laughing. "Well, so was my marriage to Matt. I guess it's fitting."

"Can't argue with that." I shrug.

"Back to Bridezilla over here." Kristin gets our attention. "I know what your motive is here, Lord Evil, but do you, the queen of design, want ugly photos? Because we're going to be in the photos, and I assure you that, no matter how much fun you're having at our expense right now, it won't be so funny on your wall."

I think about that for a second, but I'm not so sure. I'm really fucking evil at times. There may be a time I regret it, but I really don't think I will. In twenty years, I can see me looking up at it and laughing at how much fun it was to put them through a sliver of the hell they put me through.

"Nope. I'm pretty sure it'll be just as funny then," I tell her and wave to the clerk. "Miss? Can we get these online if you don't have enough here?"

Revenge is a dish best served with ugly bridesmaid dresses.

"It's almost time," Dad says as he enters the dressing room area. "Are you ready?"

I had no intentions of letting him walk me down the aisle. None. However, my mother's need for status and decorum demanded it. I was totally fine making the walk all by my damn self, just like I've done most of my life.

The idea of him acting like a father and "giving me away" is comical. He has never been much of a father to me.

Again, I gave Esther the reins, and I must allow her to lead the horse.

"Sure, Dad."

"So, you really want to do this?"

"Umm . . ."

"I'm just saying, marriage and Dupree don't exactly go hand in hand. Now is the last chance to back out."

He can't be fucking serious. "Really, Dad?"

"Did you guys do a prenup?"

"Daddy!" I yell. "Seriously, it's my wedding day. We're not having this conversation."

He shrugs as though he has no idea why I could be irritated. "I just want to make sure you're protected from this guy."

I roll my eyes. Callum has about ten times more money than I do, owns two companies, and is far more established in the business world. My father is ridiculous. If someone looked at this from the outside, it would look like I trapped Callum instead of the other way around.

I mean . . . I would totally jump to that conclusion.

"You never gave a shit about me before, why now?"

His head jerks back. "What the hell are you talking about? You're my daughter."

"Yes. I am, but it's not like we have a relationship. Now you're suddenly concerned about my marriage and financial future?"

My dad's face pales. "I'm really sorry you think that way, Nicole. I've always loved you. I just didn't know that you didn't know that."

Do not cry now. Do not cry now.

"You've always been distant. It felt like you only came around when it would piss Mom off."

He steps forward and pulls me into his arms. I can count on one hand how many times my father has hugged me. The first was when I was six and he told me he was leaving. I clung to him like a barnacle on the hull of a ship, refusing to come off no matter how hard he scraped. The second was when my dog died. I was totally inconsolable. The last time was when my grandma died, and again, I was a crying mess at the funeral. His mother was the sweetest woman. She was warm and loving. I never really understood how he came from her.

Never was it really him who initiated it.

"I never knew you felt that way."

"How could you not?" A tear forms, and I fan my face.

He sighs. "I always thought it was you who felt angry with me for leaving when you were a little girl."

"Of course, I was angry, but I really just wanted you to come around more. For being married so many times, you really suck at knowing what women want."

My dad laughs a few times and shakes his head. "Maybe that's why I keep losing them . . ."

"Could be."

A knock on the door breaks up this weird moment. "Almost time," Kristin says with a smile. "You ready?"

"I'm ready."

"Last chance . . ." Dad says again.

I roll my eyes and place my hand in the crook of his elbow. "Let's go before I change my mind about letting you walk next to me."

He chuckles. "Well, you look beautiful."

"Thanks, Daddy."

"I'm proud of you."

I squeeze his arm a little. "I'm really happy."

"I'm glad. You look a lot like your mother did on our wedding day. Happy, full of hope, and practically glowing."

There must be some kind of cosmic thing happening because that almost sounded as if he was complimenting her.

"Well, weddings can do that to her," I try to joke it off because I'm slightly worried he's been taken over by a ghost.

"Yes, she sure does love her weddings," he says as we exit the small room.

Nerves start to swirl inside me. I'm getting married to Callum today. I'm going to be a wife to someone. This man must be nuts for thinking this is a good idea. What if he has buyer's remorse? What if he realizes I'm really a lot crazier than he knows at this point? What if all the things he thinks are cute now become annoying and he smothers me with a pillow? Or worse . . . I smother him.

I don't want to go to jail.

We get to the door, and I'm shaking. My father places his hand over mine, which is a good thing since I'm pretty sure I'm about to lose the use of my legs.

Fight or flight. Fight or flight.

The doors open with me still standing here, and all the feelings that were swirling around me stop the minute I see him.

He's standing at the end of the blush-pink runner with thousands of petals all around. His back is to me, but his profile is clear.

We start walking, and I look around in awe. There's silk draping along the aisle chairs, and candles line the entire area.

My mother insisted we get married around eight at night. She said there was nothing equivalent to sunset glow in photos, which I happen to know all too well.

When we turn the corner, my heart begins to race. I no longer care about the beauty of the event, the sunset, or the linens. I don't care about the people sitting in the chairs, smiling up at me. I couldn't give two shits less about anything other than Callum.

It's so cliché because I always thought people were ridiculous when they said it.

But I get it now that I'm here.

Love is a fairy tale inside you. It lives there, telling the story of all that's to come if you can just remember the words. Love is a living thing that we have to nurture when times are bad.

I see that now.

Because with Callum, it's true love.

"Mrs. Huxley, or can I call you Mom now?" I ask my new mother-in-law while we're standing there for photos.

"Mrs. Huxley is just fine."

She freaking hates me. Hates. Like with the fiery pits of hell kind of hate. Not only did I steal her perfect son but also I made him move to America.

Me. It's *all* me.

It isn't as if he hadn't already had it planned before any of that. Nope. It's me. The devil incarnate. I've given up trying to change her mind. I'm well aware that is never going to happen. For now, I'd settle for her just to tolerate me—for his sake.

"Okay, then. I just wanted to see if maybe we can have a few photos together."

"What for?"

So I can throw darts at them?

"Well, I know Callum is really torn up about being away from you. I had offered to go to London," I toss it in for good measure, "but he insisted this was where he really needed to be since Dove-tail is now his. Plus, I just think it would be something nice he could put on his desk, don't you think? He can see the two most important women in his life. It would really make him happy."

If I hadn't used the Callum card, I'm one hundred percent sure she would've told me to fuck off in the politest way possible. She seems to be really good at that.

"If you think Callum would like it, then I guess we can take *one* photo."

Gee, thanks.

"Wonderful," I say as though she just gave me a check for a million bucks.

I wave to our photographer, and he rushes over. I explain that I'd like a few photos of me and his mother for Callum, and he takes us over to another spot on the grounds that has some beautiful scenery.

She doesn't say much, probably because she's plotting my death, but whatever.

I appreciate that she's taking the photos, and this way, at least I can say that I tried.

"Thank you, Mrs. Huxley."

"There's nothing I wouldn't do for *my* child. Sacrificing one's happiness is often a part of motherhood. Including having to get on a plane to come back to the one place that had caused me so much pain since *you* wouldn't have the wedding in London, but for my son, I did it."

I nod. "I hope you know that I feel the same about him and the baby."

You'd think she'd like me a little considering I am pregnant with her grandchild.

"I guess time will tell, dear." Her voice is filled with skepticism.

I'm a pretty chill person, at least I'd like to think so, and I get that I'm no mother's dream for their child, but I love Callum. I married the asshat, I am having his baby, and I told him to keep his three million bucks because I'd design his entire life for free.

This should have garnered me at least a bit of trust from her. *Should have.*

"I know you don't know me," I start off with my voice soft. "I know that I'm just some American girl who got pregnant, came to London, and then left without a word. There's no denying I'm not your first choice." She starts to cut me off, but I keep going. "I would just ask you to give me a chance. I love your son very much. I want to make him happy, and I know that he loves you, and it means a lot to us for you to accept me."

Mrs. Huxley takes a step forward. She places her hand on my cheek. "Bring him back to London and that would help." Her hand drops, and I stand here stunned.

Mothers. They always make me crazy.

thirty-three

. . .

Callum

"MAY I HAVE THIS DANCE, LOVE?" I ask my beautiful wife.

"Of course, husband."

I pull her to my side and walk to the center of the dance floor. Nicole has always been beautiful, but today, she's exquisite.

Nothing will ever compare to this moment.

"I'm sorry your brother couldn't be here," she says as I hold her in my arms.

I tried to hide it, but it bothers me. I didn't have a best man who I grew up with. I'd always thought it would be him standing beside me. Although, he was there for the first wedding. Still, this wedding is different. Nicole is different.

"I got to have Eli Walsh and Noah Frazier as my wedding party. I think I fared better than most."

"This is true. I mean . . . you'll probably be on the cover of some tabloid since both of them were here."

"What I've always wanted in life . . ."

"Still, I'm sorry that he didn't come."

I appreciate that she feels that way. Nicole isn't usually soft about these things. I almost expected her to call him a prick and an arsehole, but she seems sad about it. "Milo is who he is. I hope one day we can find a way to be close again."

"I hope so too."

"You know, we weren't always this way. For a while, we were best friends. He was going to take a much higher leadership role in the company, but something happened and he just got almost resentful of anything I had. I thought maybe we'd get on, find a way to rebuild whatever bridge was torn down, but it never happened. Still, I can't change it, all I can do is be happy I have you right now."

I have very little understanding of what caused the rift between us. I know he's always hated that I was technically his boss.

She nods. "Your mother seems to . . . you know . . . not be shooting death stares at me for the moment."

"She'll warm to you."

Hopefully.

Mum flew here last week, wanting to spend a bit of time with Nicole before the big day. I hoped the two women I love would get on, but I think Nicole scares Mum. She asked me several times if I was thinking straight, and then I put my foot down, explaining that Nicole was my choice.

"At least our mothers seem to like each other," she notes whilst looking over.

"Yes, they're getting on quite well."

Nicole laughs. "I'm going to be so sad when your accent fades and you're saying things like, yo, yo what's up?"

I shake my head. "I don't think I'll ever say that."

"You never know. I can get my gangster on with the best of them."

"Good to know. So, I take it our child will be exposed to all kinds of music?"

Her fingers play with the hair on my nape. "Absolutely. First, their uncle is Eli Walsh, so of course, they'll know about boy bands. Then, we have you ... who thinks rock is the only acceptable music, which is not true. I have to round him out with some DMX, Biggie, and 2Pac. It's really important our kid be well versed in the rap genre."

I laugh at her reasoning. "Well, good thing the kids will also get some Kenny G, Prince, and Eric Clapton."

"Kids? As in plural?"

"Yes. Kids."

I want many children. I want us to fill our home with toys, laughter, and the sound of little feet.

Nicole laughs. "You're on the one and done plan, honey."

"The what?"

"One kid, and we're done."

"We'll discuss that at another time."

Her face tells me there really is no discussion left to have, but I'll find my way to convince her.

"Have you had a good day?" I ask as I twirl her around the dance floor.

"It's been the best. You?"

"I've never been happier in my life, and it's all because of you."

She smiles and then rests her head on my chest. "I love you, Cal."

"I love you, Nic."

Her eyes meet mine at the use of her nickname, and she giggles. "You know, I was totally going to let you put it in my butt, but now ..."

"I have all the plans in the world of doing it regardless. As my wife, I feel it's only right."

"Do you?"

I nod. "You promised to give me all of you."

"That I did. But remember, babe, you did the same."

What the hell does that mean?

The sound of people clanging forks against their glasses fills the room, stopping me from asking her. Nicole smiles and looks up at me. "That means they want us to kiss."

"Kiss?"

"Yes, so put your lips to mine," she demands.

Far be it from me to pass up the opportunity to kiss her. I don't need others to ask for it, but this is one American custom I can get behind. If all I need to do is tap a glass, I can handle that.

I pull Nicole closer and then dip her back. Her arms wrap around my neck as I cradle her. Then, I lay a deep kiss on her lips. It's one of those camera moments that I hope someone has the wherewithal to capture.

epilogue

. . .

Nicole

~eight months later~

"I HATE YOU! I hate you so much! I hope your balls fall off!" I scream as another contraction hits.

This fucking kid wouldn't come out. I know I'm great and all, but she's two weeks late. Two very long weeks in which I've been miserable, perpetually hot, and incapable of being more than five minutes away from the bathroom. As if that wasn't bad enough, I haven't seen my crotch in months and now some doctor is elbow deep in there.

I want to die.

"You're doing wonderful," Callum says as he pushes my sweaty hair off my face.

"Fuck off."

I don't care if I'm doing wonderful. I had a goddamn plan. I was going to have this baby at forty weeks, push for a few hours, not really breaking a big sweat, and be able to take photos that would be ready for social media right after.

It's been sixteen hours of fucking labor, a baby the size of a toddler is trying to come out because she wanted to stay put, and I'm pretty sure I burst a blood vessel in my eye from pushing so hard.

"Deep breath, Nicole, another contraction is coming," the doctor warns. I'm so glad he wants me to breathe. Stupid men. All of them.

I turn to Callum. "I can't do this anymore. I'm done. I can't, she can just stay in there."

At twenty weeks, we got our ultrasound that said we were having a little girl. I swear, I was online ordering things before we left the parking lot. This is my dream. Her room is absolutely stunning. It is pale pink with gray and gold accents. Callum allowed me to spend whatever I wanted on her room.

Not that I wasn't going to anyway, but each time a box came, he smiled, which made me get more boxes because I didn't want to deprive my husband of his happiness.

Now, I would do anything to make her stop trying to kill me.

He shakes his head. "I don't think she wants to."

"Because you made her angry!" They did this. They induced my labor. "The kid wants to stay in, why are we forcing her to vacate the premises?"

"You wanted her out," he reminds me.

I really wish that looks could at least turn people to stone. Statues can't talk. "That was before I knew *this* was what I was asking for!"

"How much longer does she have?" he asks the doctor.

"If you can push really hard on this one, we'll have the baby's head out."

"Oh, so gross!" I complain.

"Do you want to see?" he asks Callum.

"No, he doesn't want to see!" I grip my husband's arm to stop him from heading down there.

There are no mirrors or recording devices. My vagina is a mess, and there will be no seeing it in this state.

No fucking way.

None.

He is to firmly stay out of my lower region.

I'd like him to only be there for pleasure, not when this big-ass thing is pushing its way out.

"Why not?"

"Because I told you why!"

He sighs. "Nicole, I already told you that I don't care, and I promise to still love you no matter what I see."

Yeah, he says that now, but what happens if I shit myself because, apparently, that's a thing while you're in labor. No guy can just forget that. I would much rather be safe than sorry, and I would think he would know better than to push me on this. He had to fight me to even be in the delivery room. I voted for Kristin or Danielle.

Of course, Danielle is working at Dovetail, and she said she would rather not piss Callum off by taking his spot in here and lose her job. As if he would ever fire her. She's a giant chicken shit.

Kristin tried telling me I would regret it before she admitted that she'd rather not be the target of my anger spurts.

Another giant chicken shit.

Heather wasn't an option. I love her, but she's all tough love, and I don't need that. I want nurturing and understanding while I'm in hell.

So, I'm stuck with my husband.

"If you go down there, you'll live to regret it. Try me, Callum Huxley."

He rolls his eyes and heads back up to the safe zone.

"Oh! Fuck!" I scream as the next contraction hits. "Thanks for the warning, Doc!" I give him the look I just gave Callum not too long ago.

"Just a few more pushes, Nicole."

Yeah, and then I'm going to find an ice bath because I swear my vag is on fire.

"Get it out!" I demand. I'm over this. All of it—the pregnancy, the hormones, the bloating, and the pain. I quit.

I'm the asshole who made a bet that I could do this without drugs. Again, my stupid stubborn side bit me in the ass. Guess who made that bet? Heather—now known as The Bitch.

She tried to say that there was no way that my "prissy" ass could handle labor without painkillers. Not like she's had a baby, but whatever, I still made the damn bet.

By hour ten, I was begging for the damn epidural, but I was already too far dilated. They thought it would stymie the progression. Little did they know that it was going to happen anyway just because God has a sense of humor.

"Here comes another one," Dr. I-Have-No-Heart says. "The head is out, now I want you to really push this time."

I glare at him. "I've been doing that."

Callum pushes my hair back. "You have, love. You just need to do it again, okay?"

I want to tell him no, but I know he'll find some stupid thing to say, and I don't really get a choice. I've never heard of a woman being able to actually quit childbirth. Although, if anyone could, it would be me.

"I'm so tired," I say while panting.

"I know, but she's almost here. Our little girl is coming."

"Okay."

"Okay. I'm right here."

I take the strength that he offers because I have none left. I'm completely spent.

"Push, Nicole."

I don't know where the might comes from when you have none,

but it comes from somewhere. As exhausted, beaten down, sore, and even a little shattered as I am, I know my daughter needs me. I have to find whatever I have left so I can give her what she needs.

So, I grip Callum's hand and push as hard as I can. I vaguely register people counting, but I don't focus on it. I just think of the baby. I think of Callum and how happy he's been. I think about our friends and family in the waiting room. I think of the love that Callum and I share, and that gives me the fuel to push.

"The baby is out!" I hear a nurse yell.

I drop my head back to the pillow and Callum kisses my forehead. "You did it, love. You did it."

"Where is she?" I ask, with literally zero energy left.

The nurse brings her over, placing her on my chest. "Here's your son."

That wakes me up. "What?"

"It's a boy."

I shake my head in denial. "No. No, I don't. I'm having a girl. Where's the girl?"

Callum's face is beaming with pride. "A boy?"

"No, I was cooking a little girl who was going to love pink. I . . ."

The nurse lifts the leg and, sure enough, there's a fucking penis.

Callum's big hand cups the back of the baby's head. "Hello, son."

I look over, still waiting for the girl because . . . that was what they told me. I was having a girl, damn it.

"We have a boy?" I ask again.

"We have a son."

"Shit. I guess naming him Olivia isn't going to work." I look down at my chest, touching his face.

He's perfect. He has the cutest button nose and his head is

round, not like some of my friend's kids who came out looking like a cone. His eyes open slightly but close right away.

"No, I would think not," Callum agrees.

"Hi, baby," I say to our son. "I'm your mom, you know, the one who has called you Livvy for the last few months, sorry about that."

Callum chuckles. "We didn't pick a boy name."

No, because we thought there was a body part missing. I look down at him again, and then I smile. "What about Colin?"

"Colin?"

I nod. "Yeah, it's close to your name and English."

He seems to think it over, and I clear my throat.

"Sixteen hours of labor, Callum. Sixteen."

He laughs and then kisses my lips before kissing the baby's head again. "Colin Huxley. Welcome to the world."

These two about killed me. I went to London and fell in love with the city and knew my hero had to be British.
And then ... he needed a brother.
Milo Huxley is nothing like you think and when he meets Danielle, well, he's knocked on his arse, that's for sure.
Grab If I Only Knew and see what happens when he meets his match.

***

Love these two and not ready to let go? I have an EXCLUSIVE Bonus Epilogue for you! Just keep swiping!

bonus scene

. . .

Nicole

"GRANNY!" Colin yells as he rushes toward his grandmother. The one who even after eight years thinks I'm not worthy of her son.

Whatever.

"Colin, my beautiful boy!"

Sure, she loves him.

"Mum," Callum spreads his arms wide and embraces her. "You look lovely as ever."

"Oh, you're too good to me." She looks at me with her smile that looks more like a scowl. "Nicole."

"Hello, Mum." I say and kiss her cheek. She hates that I've decided to call her Mum. If she had her way, I'd be calling her my ex-mother-in-law. But, no such luck for her. I'm here to stay.

"How was your flight?" She asks me, but then turns to the boys for the answer.

"It was great! Dad let us fly in the pods and we had so much junk food."

"Really? Well, that sounds like you have quite the father."

"And his mother is pretty wonderful too," Callum tacks on.

I don't know why he tries. There's no winning over the old bat. I'm the bad seed who hasn't allowed the prodigal son to return to London.

Not like he has a freaking empire that he runs in the States. Not like he's really freaking happy there. And of course he visits pretty much every two months, but . . . it's all my fault.

"Yes, well, what is on the agenda for this holiday?" she asks.

Callum's kisses the side of my head and wraps his arm around my shoulder. I've stopped letting it bother me a long time ago. It's really funny most of the time. I like to rile her up because she makes it so easy.

"Colin wants to go out and see more of England. I thought we'd stay in London for a day or two and then head out, maybe go to Bath or even Brighton. Then we'll head back and spend a few more days with you."

She smiles. "I love that Colin is so interested in his homeland."

Oh, look, another dig at Nicole.

Callum smiles softly. "Mum, he's very well aware he's British."

"That's my point."

"Yes, of course it was."

I look to Callum, a little shocked he actually went back at her. He's a wonderful man. A fantastic husband, father, and provider. I couldn't be any luckier than to have found him, but dear God does he cater to his mother somedays.

Maybe it's because I thrived on pissing mine off so much that it drives me crazy, but she is his weakness—and she knows it.

"Daddy," Colin says as he yawns. "I'm so tired."

Jet lag is the worst parts of these trips. It's so hard to get Colin adjusted, but we try. Five-year-old kids aren't exactly known for their patience, but put extreme exhaustion on top of it and he becomes the Devil's child.

"I'll take him up," I offer, trying to lift him.

Seriously, this kid is so freaking heavy. I don't know what the hell we're feeding him, but dear Lord.

"I want Daddy." He whines and I almost drop him.

"Daddy will be up in a second." There's no way I'm staying down here by myself. No freaking way. I'll strap the kid to my back if I have to. Pain is temporary, even if I throw my back out, it'll be better than staying down here with Mummy dearest.

"Here," Callum says as he takes Colin into his arms. "I'll take him up and you stay with him."

My husband is amazing.

"Thank you."

"Take your time, dear," his Mum says as we climb the stairs.

When we get up there, I swear my mouth is filled with blood from biting down so hard.

Callum puts Colin in his bed with his iPad. "Watch as much as you can, the longer you can stay awake, the better, remember?"

"I'll try, Dad."

"Good lad." We walk to the door, out of earshot from Colin. "I'm sorry," he says.

"It's fine. I'm used to it."

"Still, you're the best thing in my life."

I smile. "Liar."

"Not even a little bit. You," he kisses my lips. "Are my whole heart."

Well, that makes me feel better. "One day she'll see I'm not half as bad as she thinks."

He laughs. "I think she sees herself in you."

"Yeah, okay." I roll my eyes.

There's nothing remotely similar about us.

"I'm serious. She was a bit of a wild child when she was young and broke a few hearts. I'm sure she's worried you're going to break mine."

"What about you breaking mine?" I counter.

I've spent years with him going back and forth to London, and I've endured the loneliness. In all our years together, I've been a pretty good wife. I'm understanding of his job, family, travel, and everything that comes with it. When he's gone, our home feels empty, my heart less full, and then when he returns, I can breathe again. Callum is the other half of my world. There are days when there's so much love inside of me that I could burst.

He is my weakness in life.

One that makes me stronger.

"Doubtful." He smirks. "I'm the good one."

I slap his chest playfully. "Ass."

"One night here and we'll be gone."

"And of course Milo is away so I can't even have him as my shield."

My brother-in-law is me in male form. I love him. He's hilarious, smart, and loves to make his mother crazy. He takes the heat off me most of the time, but this trip, Callum made him go back to the States while we were away.

Callum laughs. "Well, you'll just have to behave."

"Like that'll ever happen."

He tilts his head to the side. "Try."

"For you . . . maybe."

Callum takes a box out of coat pocket and holds it toward me.

"What's this?" I ask.

"Look at it."

He's always doing these things. I get flowers because it's Monday, cards because he thought of me, text messages during the day because I'm on his mind, and gifts because he can't stop himself.

I'm not complaining by any means, but sometimes I don't know how to handle being treated so good.

"Callum," I say his name softly. "You didn't have to get me anything."

"But I did."

"Why?"

"Because that's what you do for someone you love. You give until you have nothing left. You love until your heart is empty and then you fill it back up again. You show them, not tell them all the things they are to you. I promised you a long time ago that I would never let you feel small."

A tear falls down my face and he wipes it away. "I love you Callum Huxley."

He kisses my forehead. "I love you Nicole Huxley."

I open the box and find a New York Yankees replica ring and laugh. "You really do know the way to my heart."

"Yes, love, Yankees and hot dogs."

I grin. "And you. Always you."

He gives me a brief kiss. "Always us. The three of us."

I look over at my son with my husband's arms around me, realizing just how freaking lucky I am.

books by corinne michaels

The Salvation Series

Beloved

Beholden

Consolation

Conviction

Defenseless

Evermore: A 1001 Dark Night Novella

Indefinite

Infinite

The Hennington Brothers

Say You'll Stay

Say You Want Me

Say I'm Yours

Say You Won't Let Go: A Return to Me/Masters and Mercenaries
Novella

Second Time Around Series

We Own Tonight

One Last Time

Not Until You

If I Only Knew

The Arrowood Brothers

Come Back for Me

Fight for Me

The One for Me

Stay for Me

Willow Creek Valley Series

Return to Us

Could Have Been Us

A Moment for Us

A Chance for Us

Rose Canyon Series

Help Me Remember (Coming 2022)

Give Me Love (Coming 2022)

Keep This Promise (Coming 2022)

Co-Written with Melanie Harlow

Hold You Close

Imperfect Match

Standalone Novels

All I Ask

You Loved Me Once

acknowledgments

If you deal with me during this process, you deserve so much more than a thank you that's back here. For real, I'm a little crazy and you know this, but . . . here it is.

To my husband and children. I don't know how you deal with me, but I can't tell you how much I appreciate you. I love you all with my whole heart.

My beta readers, Katie, Melissa, Jo : Thank you so much for your support and love during this book. I love you guys and couldn't imagine not having you. I hope I did the British parts proud.

My assistant, Christy Peckham: When I say I hate you, I'm totally lying. I love you so much. I'll totally deny this.

My readers. There's no way I can thank you enough. It still blows me away that you read my words. You guys are everything to me. Everything.

Bloggers: You're the heart and soul of this industry. Thank you for choosing to read my books and fit me into your insane schedules. I appreciate it more than you know.

Ashley, my editor, for always pushing me to write outside of my comfort zone.. Janice and Michele for proofreading and making sure each detail is perfect!

Melanie Harlow, thank you for being the good witch in our duo or Ethel to my Lucy. Your friendship means the world to me and I love writing with you (especially when you let me kill characters.)

Bait, Stabby, and Corinne Michaels Books – I love you more than you'll ever know.

My agent, Kimberly Brower, I am so happy to have you on my team. Thank you for your guidance and support.

Melissa Erickson, you're amazing. I love your face.

about the author

Corinne Michaels is a New York Times, USA Today, and Wall Street Journal bestselling author of romance novels. Her stories are chock full of emotion, humor, and unrelenting love, and she enjoys putting her characters through intense heartbreak before finding a way to heal them through their struggles.

Corinne is a former Navy wife and happily married to the man of her dreams. She began her writing career after spending months away from her husband while he was deployed—reading and writing were her escapes from the loneliness. Corinne now lives in Virginia with her husband and is the emotional, witty, sarcastic, and fun-loving mom of two beautiful children.

CPSIA information can be obtained
at www.ICGtesting.com
Printed in the USA
BVHW061744260422
635319BV00004B/128

9 781942 834960